Gidget

Gidget

THE LITTLE GIRL WITH BIG IDEAS

a novel by
FREDERICK KOHNER

The original hardcover <u>Gidget</u>, published in 1957. That's Kathy Kohner holding her board for a bitchen bestseller!

Gidget

Frederick Kohner

Foreword by
Kathy Kohner Zuckerman
* aka the real Gidget *

Introduction by
Deanne Stillman

BERKLEY BOOKS, NEW YORK

A Berkley Book
Published by The Berkley Publishing Group
A division of Penguin Putnam Inc.
375 Hudson Street
New York, New York 10014

Copyright © 1957 by Frederick Kohner.
Foreword copyright © 2001 by Kathy Kohner Zuckerman.
Introduction copyright © 2001 by Deanne Stillman.
Outer cover photographs by Ernest Lenart.
Inside front cover photographs—top row: photos courtesy of Kathy
Kohner Zuckerman; second row: photo by Ernest Lenart; third row: left photo
by Ernest Lenart, right photo copyright © by Warren Miller Photo;
bottom row: photo by Surf Photos by Grannis.
Inside back cover photographs—top row: photos by Ernest Lenart;
second row: left photo by Ernest Lenart, right photo courtesy of the
Frederick Kohner Estate; third row: photo courtesy of Kathy Kohner
Zuckerman; bottom row: photo copyright © by Warren Miller Photo.
Text design by Tiffany Kukec.

PRINTING HISTORY
First published in the U.S.A. in 1957
Published in Great Britain by Michael Joseph in 1958
Penguin Books hardcover edition / 1963
Berkley trade paperback edition / June 2001

The Penguin Putnam Inc. World Wide Web site address is
www.penguinputnam.com

Library of Congress Cataloging-in-Publication Data

Kohner, Frederick.
    Gidget / Frederick Kohner : foreword by Kathy Kohner Zuckerman :
introduction by Deanne Stillman.
        p. cm.
    ISBN 0-425-17962-1
    1. Teenage girls—Fiction. 2. Malibu (Calif.)—Fiction. 3. Beaches—Fiction.
4. Surfing—Fiction. I. Title.

PS3521.O334 G5 2001
813'.54—dc21
                                                        2001029508

PRINTED IN THE UNITED STATES OF AMERICA

20 19 18 17 16 15 14

To the Gidget
with love

Foreword

I was eight or nine years old when I saw my first surfboard. My family lived in a quiet neighborhood in Brentwood, California, and my mother would regularly give two teenage boys who lived down the street a ride to Malibu beach. They would place their giant surfboards in the backseat (I used to call it the "rumbleseat" of our Model-A Ford). Their names were Matt Kivlin and Buzzy Trent, and they were the first surfers I ever met.

While in my early teens, my folks used to take me with them to Malibu on a regular basis. My mom always insisted I come along, even though at the age of fifteen I found going to the movie theaters more appealing. But she would never allow me to sit inside a dark movie theater on a beautiful day. She always made me go to the beach on those sunny weekends. She was adamant that the beach would be more fun and entertaining, and much healthier for me. How right she was. Of course, at the time, I thought she was mean.

Going to Malibu with my folks generally meant sitting

around with them and their friends—very boring. So I would wander up the beach, taking long walks, and it was on one of those long walks, one day, that I came upon the surfers who dwelled beside Malibu Pier. Watching them ride the waves was incredible. I immediately decided to buy a surfboard and try my best to learn the art of surfing.

I bought my first surfboard from Mike Doyle for thirty dollars and hit the water. I wasn't really sure what I was doing, but I watched the "boys" on their boards and imitated as best I could the "sport." I also started to socialize with this small group of surfers—mostly male—and actually became rather fascinated with their way of life. It was a most alluring lifestyle, especially to a fifteen-year-old girl. They were boys who lived on the beach (literally in a shack on the sand). They all had nicknames. One day I was referred to as Gidget (girl-midget)—and just like that, I was the Gidget. I was amused and fascinated with these handsome young surfers and their love and pure devotion to riding the waves at Malibu. It seemed as if there wasn't any other aspect to their lives except taking in the sun and sea, waxing down their boards, and paddling out looking for a great wave to catch. This was their life—nothing else. It was its own culture and we all knew one another—we knew everyone who had a surfboard, and there weren't very many of us!! I felt like I had a new family, and I was the girl midget. I was the Gidget!

It was the summer of 1956. I was in the tenth grade. I had fallen in love with surfboard riding. I couldn't wait to get to Malibu every day that summer of my fifteenth year. I knew this was true fun in the sun, but also hard work, too—learning to surfboard ride, that is.

I was totally enthralled with my new passion and my new group of friends, and I kept telling my dad and mom about the whole experience—about the waves and the "kuks" (that was what the surfers were called) at Malibu.

One day I told my dad that I wanted to write a story about my summer days at Malibu: about my friends who lived in a shack on the beach, about the major crush I had on one of the surfers, about how I was teased, about how hard it was to catch a wave—to paddle the long board out—and how persistent I was at wanting to learn to surf and to be accepted by the "crew," as I often referred to the boys that summer.

My father, Frederick Kohner, was a Hollywood screenwriter at the time. He became absorbed and amused with my tales of the beach. He told me he would write the story for me. He wrote the book *Gidget* in six weeks. It was his first novel. It became a best-seller and the basis for subsequent popular movies and television shows.

Though based on my personal experience, *Gidget* is a work of fiction. It is a wonderful story; the story of a young girl, like myself, who learns on her own the great sport of surfboard riding and the art of persistence and doing something she really wants to do even though at the time there were very few girl surfers doing it. And it was not easy. The original hardcover edition of *Gidget* has now become a collector's item, and I'm really thrilled that you'll be reading the story again, or for the first time. I've always loved the book. And I think you will, too.

There's never been a time when I haven't loved the beach. I have always loved watching the surfers, wherever they are. I loved my days at Malibu. I surfed the summers of '56, '57, and

'58. In '58 I went away to college at Oregon State, but I continued to ride the long boards through the summers of '59 and '60.

Five years ago I went surfing again with Mike Doyle, from whom I bought my first surfboard over forty years ago. It was a wonderful day, though I haven't been back in the water since. But now that *Gidget* is back—the real Gidget will be back, too. Who says sixty-year-old Gidgets can't ride the waves anymore?

I hope you love the book and go out and "hang ten" (an old surfing expression).

Thanks for reading it. Keep paddling.

Love,

Kathy (Gidget) Kohner Zuckerman

Kathy Kohner Zuckerman works as a restaurant hostess in California and lives close enough to the beach to hear the waves, if she listens closely. She turned sixty in January 2001.

Introduction
by Deanne Stillman

When Kathy Kohner Zuckerman talks about Malibu, California, she is referring to life at Malibu Point from 1956 to 1959, a hallowed surf-warp when legendary figures such as the Beetle, the Bucker, the Jaw, Quik, Golden Boy, Turtle, Moondoggie, Mysto, Steak, Scooter, Fencer, and the Cat adopted Kathy, a precocious teenager, into the tribe and named her as they did the others, for her most notable characteristics. She was a girl, one of the few who surfed at the time, and at five feet tall and ninety-five pounds, she was a midget. Unto us, the sea nymph, Gidget, was born.

In surfing parlance, the wave at Malibu—twenty miles from downtown Los Angeles—is as good as it gets. It runs for about four hundred yards, from the pier where the old, abandoned hulk of Alice's Restaurant sits, northward to the mouth of Malibu Lagoon, which is just south of Malibu Colony, now a private celebrity enclave. There are actually three surf breaks here—First Point, Second Point, and Third Point. A south-facing beach,

Malibu is situated and configured in a way that causes the New Zealand storm swells of summer to break in waves that are consistent, perfectly formed, gentle, and, on the outside points, fast. Extensive kelp beds keep the surface glassy and smooth. The surf is rarely above eight feet, most often from two to four. Sometimes a ride can last as long as two minutes. Malibu was named by the Chumash Indians ten thousand years ago; the original *hu-mal-iwu* translates as "it makes a loud noise all the time over there."

Some time ago, I had heard from friends in the surf community that there was an actual person named Gidget—not the character who appeared in the many movies and television series whose titles bore her name, often in conjunction with the phrase " ... Goes to ... " or "The New ... " and always set on the beach in the most goofy and innocent of ways. In an age of few surprises, the fact that Gidget really existed was indeed news, and I wanted to meet the person whose name was forever associated with riding waves. After several telephone calls, I located Gidget and asked for an interview. I did not have to chart my way through handlers, publicists, or agents. Kathy Kohner Zuckerman invited me to meet her in her home.

"We were living in Brentwood," Kathy recalled one day on her patio near the sea. "My mother used to drive some of the neighborhood guys down to the beach. They would put their boards in her Model-A. I tagged along. I wanted to surf. It looked like so much fun. I remember asking one of the surfers if I was bothering him. He said, 'You're breathing, aren't you?' There was this guy named Steak living in a shack. A few other surfers were always hanging around. They were always hungry. I think some of them lived there too." The shack that Gidget referred to is legendary: although long-gone, like its fellow sacred Malibu spot known as "the pit," its very mention among surfers, especially those who surfed Malibu in the fifties, conjures a mythology that forever binds the tribe.

Kathy continued. Every day, she said, she would bring a paper sack of homemade sandwiches and trade them for the use of someone's surfboard. Soon, she bought her own board from a fifteen-year-old named Mike Doyle, later a well-known shaper, for thirty dollars. "It was blue and had a totempole on it," she said. "I wish I still had it."

It was perhaps inevitable that Kathy's father, Frederick Kohner, became fascinated with the stories that his daughter would tell him about the beach. He and his two brothers grew up in the Czechoslovakian spa town of Teplitz-Schonau (whose tainted waters Ibsen wrote about in his famous play about a corrupt spa called *Enemy of the People*). Their father, Julius, was the proprietor of the local movie house. In 1921, Paul, the eldest son, joined the early wave of Jewish emigrés and left for Hollywood where he became an agent. After receiving his Ph.D. from the University of Vienna, Frederick, the middle son, embarked on a career as a screenwriter in Berlin. In 1936, to escape Hitler, he left Germany with his wife, Fritzie, first for London and then, after Paul got him a writing deal at Columbia, for Hollywood.

Within a few years, Frederick Kohner established himself as a well-respected screenwriter, working at all the major studios, writing and selling more than twenty screenplays, one of which, *Mad About Music*, was nominated for an Academy Award. In addition, he penned two Broadway plays, *The Bees and the Flowers* and *Stalin Allee* and, after the success of *Gidget*, fifteen other books, including *Cher Papa* and *Kiki of Montparnasse*.

The family settled in Brentwood, a twenty-minute ride from the beach. In 1956, at the age of fifteen, Gidget began spending all of her free time at Malibu—after school, after work, on weekends, or when her family was visiting friends in the Malibu Colony. "My father and I would walk down," she said, "and I would tell him about all of the surfers. I told him I wanted to write a book. He said, 'Why don't you tell me your stories and I'll write it?' I said 'Okay.'"

And thus Gidget became her father's muse, recounting tales of "bitchen surf" and giant "combers" that rolled in from Japan.

Frederick was the best of students, fascinated, paying careful attention to his daughter's language (German was his first), and even—with her permission—listening in on her telephone conversations. Enchanted by the surf that was breaking at his doorstep, he wrote the novel in six weeks, weaving Gidget's accounts and conversation into a charming fiction which reflected the concerns of the day. The narrative explores the perennial American theme—whether to drop out of society's mainstream or live the expected life—through Gidget's enchantment with two male characters, the Kahoona and Moondoggie. But another theme resounds above all others in the novel—Kathy's passion for wave-riding. "The great Kahoona," says the fictional Gidget, "showed me the first time how to get on my knees, to push the shoulders up and slide the body back—to spring to your feet quickly, putting them a foot apart and under you in one motion. That's quite tricky. But then, surf-riding is not playing Monopoly and the more I got the knack of it, the more I was crazy about it and the more I was crazy about it, the harder I worked at it." This is as concise a description of how to surf that I have come across, serving me well in my own surf endeavors over the years.

At the end of this sweet summer's tale, as Moondoggie confronts the Kahoona over what appears to be a scene of consummated passion, Gidget takes off on her board. It's a classic day with bitchen surf. In fact, some very big waves are rolling in. In an epic moment that has been lost in the countless Gidget remakes and retellings, in a moment that makes this novel a long-lost *Catcher in the Rye* for girls, Gidget ignores the warnings of her men and continues paddling out to sea, defying social convention—not heading back to the sanctuary of land and the expected middle-class life that it promised, not interested in whether she can hook up with a beach bum or a fraternity boy, just wanting to surf, confident that she can ride with the best of 'em. "Shoot the curl," the boys call, once she's up and cruising. "Shoot it, Gidget." And shoot it she does.

The little surf saga was now complete, and a deal was instantly hatched. The book hit the racks and critics hailed Kohner's work for its authentic evocation of a curious subculture, and some marvelled at how a foreign writer became so facile with American slang. Within several years, surfing exploded; who better to spread the word than the father of the water sprite Kathy/Gidget, a man who had fled central Europe, charmed by waves and those who found freedom by riding them?

As Gidget recalled the story, she unveiled a treasure: old scrapbooks and diaries—documents that have become the holy grail of contemporary surf culture, rumored by certain surfers to exist, and said to be the very visual and written proof that the voice which spoke through Frederick Kohner's engaging hand was indeed his daughter's. Here was news of a sweeter time, here was the gee-whiz and goofy voice of Gidget that through her father had memorialized Malibu forever and propelled the culture on a never-ending ride:

"July twenty-second, 1956. I went to the beach again today . . . I just love it down there . . . I went out surfing about three times but only caught one wave.

"June sixteenth, 1957. Boy was it a fabulous day today. Everyone was at the beach. I rode a wave today and everybody saw me.

"August third, 1957. Boy the surf was so bitchen today I couldn't believe it . . . I got some real good rides from inside."

By 1958, all things Malibu had changed—the secret was out. The waves once surfed by a few locals were now the destination for all who would be tan and cool. Southern California was transformed forever and so, in turn, was the rest of the country as an endless summer of surf music and culture would begin to defy the course of the sun and sweep eastward across the mountains and prairies and waters, eastward as far as the opposite coast and then around the world until soon, as the Beach Boys would sing, everybody had "gone surfin', surfin' USA." In her entry of June thirtieth of that year, Gidget, innocent of the great social change to come, entered a notation in her diary that, like the others, was a simple observation of a day at the beach: "Went and saw them film the [*Gidget*] movie," she wrote, " . . . It's really funny."

Some time later, I accompanied Gidget on a return to Malibu. It was a perfect day, not too crowded. "Good waves," Gidget said.

"Jeeze, did you see that?" She took off her sandals as we walked past the pit and toward the now-vacant site of the shack, her old haunts, sandy repositories of powerful tribal crosscurrents not detectable by outsiders. "Oh, my God," Gidget said. "There's Mysto." Mysto had been surfing Malibu since 1954, never missing a good day, long after many of Kathy's contemporaries had drifted away. In full wetsuit and neoprene cap, Mysto with the blazing, sea-blue eyes that only certain surfers seem to have, was carrying his dinged-up longboard, ready to paddle back out. "Looks bitchen," Kathy said. "Yeah," he said. "You wanna surf?" Kathy said that for the first time in years, she was thinking about it. Later that day, she took her board to the shop for repairs. A few days after that, a special commemorative issue of *Surfer Magazine* hit the stands. Kathy was listed as number seven of the twenty-five most important surfers of the century, one of two women to make the cut, ranking high in the surf community's "Book of Numbers," not too far below Duke Kahanomoku, adored Hawaiian father of modern surfing.

Some say it was Hollywood that lured certain emigres from afar. Perhaps. I like to think it was the waves. Were it not for Frederick Kohner and the settling of his family near the Southern California coast, the secrets of Malibu would have been lost to memory, to the endless surf, to the ancient Chumash whose spirits are said to patrol the waters, whose counsel and appeasement is sought by those who yearn for a return to the era when it was just a small band of compadres who surfed here by day and made bonfires at night, talking in hushed tones of bitchen surf and all the waves that were sure to come, all the briny wonders that would unveil themselves in their own sweet time to those who wanted to see, and to see again. And so, here, in a brand-new century and era, is the charming novel known as *Gidget*—the first, and last, word on a mythological figure who eagerly paddled these magic waters and shared the joy with her father, who in turn chronicled the tale for posterity, and all the girls who might someday hop on a wave and ride it.

Deanne Stillman is a widely published and anthologized writer. Her work appears in the New York Times, Los Angeles Times, Salon.com *and other publications. Her prizewinning play* Pray for Surf *has been produced in theaters around the country.*

**Kathy and her dad, Frederick Kohner,
the author of <u>Gidget</u>.**

Photo courtesy of the Frederick Kohner Estate

One

I'm writing this down because I once heard that when you're getting older you're liable to forget things and I'd sure be the most miserable woman in this world if I ever forgot what happened this summer. It's probably a lousy story and can't hold up a candle to those French novels from Sexville, but it has one advantage: it's a true story on my word of honor. On the other hand, a true story might not be a good story. That's what my English-comp teacher says—Mr. Glicksberg that barfy-looking character who's practically invented halitosis. But then, he is dishing out a lot of bilge water if you ask me and what does a creep of an English teacher know about writing, anyhow? Just to give you an idea of how these guys figure you can become a writer, they tell you things like this—or at least that character Glicksberg does—quote: "To begin your description of a place take pencil and a notebook, sit down at your window (or on the crest of a hill, or the bank of a river) and jot down bits of description." Unquote Glicksberg!

I tried it. I was sort of desperate to write this story so I drove out to the main drag (I got my junior license only last week) all by myself, and I took that pencil and notebook along and was all set to begin at the beginning. I mean with the description of the place. It was a bitchen day, too. The sun was out and all that, even though it was near the end of November. But then, we are living in Southern California and if you wouldn't look at the calendar you'd hardly know the difference—honest! Except that it gets dark around five in November . . . and quicker than a witch's bat.

I could have driven those twelve miles out past the main drag with a mask around my eyes like on *What's My Line?* when they try to figure out the mystery guest, on account of having gone out there at least millions of times this summer and the summers before except those before don't count. "Out there" means old Malibu.

Now, right here I have to stop. You say "Malibu" and immediately you think of the movie colony and the snazzy beach houses—and James Mason wading into the sundown on account of being a has-been and all. That's not the Malibu I'm writing about. What I mean is that one small bay along the twenty-seven miles of Rancho Malibu right next to the pier where the waves coming from Japan crash against the shore like some bitchen rocket bombs. Sometimes, that is. There is only one other place along the coast where they have that kind of incredible power and that is down south at San Onofre. When you graduate from Malibu you move down to San Onofre or Tressle where the real big humps come blasting in . . . and once you've licked those there is only one step further to Makaha where they have the real giant wetbacks. But that's in Hawaii. I've seen those boomers in a movie and I'm telling you they'd damn near kill you just seeing them on the screen. Real big deal.

But I'm getting all out of focus. That's the trouble with writing. You mention something like old Malibu and some waves and you ooze out all over the place and forget what you wanted to say. "You must organize your material! Have a point of view"— that's what old Glicksberg said. He's probably right, too. If I don't organize I'll never get my story on paper. Like my girlfriend, Mai Mai Richardson. She wants to be a playwright, but never gets beyond the description of a place. The description is really elaborate . . . about six typewritten pages and by that time, she's lost her desire to go into dialogue.

Well, to come back to that small bay near the pier where all this started, it was just the right day to drive out there and cuddle up with pencil and notebook. I parked the car near the pier and walked out to the end of it where all those nice and seedy-looking people stand and chuck their fishing rods into the breakwaters. Boy, it sure was a great day! The seagulls were circling and the pelicans executed some of their power dives, coming up again with nothing in particular to show for it.

At the end of the pier I sat down on one of the benches and looked over to the strip of beach that had been my whole life last summer. It looked quite depressing now with all the props knocked out of the picture, like an abandoned stage set. Gone was the Quonset hut of the great Kahoona, gone the red and blue color specks of the gay sailboats, and frantically I tried to conjure up the faces and voices of the "Go-Heads of Malibu." Where were they now—"Golden Boy Charlie," "Hot Shot Harrison," "Schweppes," "Don Pepe," "Scooterboy Miller," "Lord Gallo," "Malibu Mac"? Up at or down at Hermosa Beach for some winter surfing? It was as if the waves had washed them away—or like they had never been there.

"When you're ready to write, choose from the many details you have jotted down . . . those that suggest the mood of the place the moment you observed it." That would be the next step. Jeez, all I had observed so far were some crummy seagulls, some pelicans and some desperate characters trying to get some fish on their hook for a lousy fish dinner or such. I guess all this comp stuff that teachers like Glicksberg try to teach you is for the birds.

So the longer I sat there and thought about this writing business, the more I realized it wasn't for me. First of all, my vocabulary is really terrible and if I tried to use all those expensive words they wouldn't be mine and besides, as I've pointed out, all I want to do is not to forget when I'm an old hag like Mrs. Hotchkiss down the street, with nothing to show for a long life but forty-five bucks of Social Security a month and crippling arthritis.

I bet old people have forgotten how it was and that goes for my parents too—even though they're not *too* ancient. They have oodles of photo albums with pictures taken when they were young—from the mountains and the lakes and the forests where they were together (mostly in Europe). Jeez, they did look happy. In the photos I mean. Maybe they were, too. But now they're married for umpteen years and real antiques and the way they sometimes snap at each other I can't figure they've been in love, ever. Maybe it's just the years. That's the way I figure it. I always thought that Philemon and Baucis stuff is just a lot of bilge water . . . I really do.

Malibu, 1945. Kathy with her mom and dad, before she started thinking about boys and surfing.

Two

I'm just crazy about swimming. I really am. I must have been thrown into some Southern California swimming pool when I was six months old, and I've been in the water ever since.

Pools are not the real thing of course. But give me a mountain lake (like the one on the Brenner Pass I swam in last year in Europe) or the Garda Lake or that bitchen Mondsee in Austria—even Lake Arrowhead. Boy, they're doing it to me.

But the real thing is the ocean. And I don't mean that crummy Adriatic Ocean and I don't mean the Atlantic either (I tried them all out). I mean the Pacific. I've been in and out of that bitchen Pacific from Carmel down to Coronado and there's no water around the world that can beat it. That's what Rachel Carson says too, and she ought to know, having written that terrific book *The Sea Around Us*.

I guess the whole thing started because I'm so short. I'm not quite five feet but if it hadn't been for that year-round swimming I'd probably stayed a dwarf. My mother had this crazy idea that I'd grow if I'd only stretch my body as much and long as possible and that's why she made me swim from the time I can remember. She took a boat up at Arrowhead Lake and I had to swim close to her as she rowed and rowed—for hours. Turned out to be not such a crazy idea after all. Most of her friends laughed at it and so did Dr. Rossman who is our family doctor, but—lo and behold—what started out as a dwarf grew into an almost five-footer. When someone asks me about my height, I always say five foot, naturally, like when someone wants to know my age, I say going on seventeen.

I was sixteen last month.

I'm really quite cute. I've real blond hair and wear it in a horsetail. My two big canines protrude a little, which worries my parents a great deal. They urge me to have my teeth pushed back with the help of some crummy piece of hardware, but I've been resisting any attempt to tamper with my personality. The only thing that worries me is my bosom. It's there all right and it sure looks good when I'm undressed, but I have a hard time making it count in a sweater or such. Most of those kids in Franklin High are a lot taller and have a lot more to show, but most of them wear those damn falsies that stick out all over the place and I'd rather be caught dead than be a phony about a thing like your bosom. Imagine what a boy thinks of you once he finds out. And he finds out sure as hell the first time he takes you to a show.

It's different in a bathing suit of course. Nothing helps there—no falsies or such phony stuff.

I've got a couple of real sexy-looking bathing suits that're pretty low-cut and have skintight fit. When Jeff saw me the first time, I was wearing the pink one and that's why he called me Pinky—real corny.

Now that I've mentioned his name I'd better stick with him for it's Jeff's story as well as mine and, when I think back to that summer and all those things that happened it'll be Jeff first and then a long, long stretch of nothing and then Cass, the great Kahoona, or maybe it will be Cass first and Cass last—who knows what comes first to your mind once you sport a lot of bags under your eyes?

Well, that day—it was the Fourth of July—I went with my parents to good old Malibu. They go there all year long on account of me liking to swim and then on account of *them* being sort of nuts about sun and fresh air and a lot of running around to "keep fit." They always meet with a bunch of other fresh-air fiends and loll around and talk a lot of boring stuff, intellectual and such, my old man being a professor of German Literature at U.S.C.

Most of the time I take a girlfriend along when I ride out to the beach with them—Mai Mai or Poppy or Barbara—but this Fourth of July I was alone. Everyone was afraid of traffic and accidents and sunstroke (we had some two hundred degrees of heat that day)—so I was good and stuck with the old lady and the old man. I took my portable radio along though and heaps of peanut butter sandwiches and *Love Is Eternal* which I have been reading on and off for a year. I'm really horrible about reading. It's embarrassing, especially for my old man who is a doctor of literature, but it just seems impossible for me to concentrate. To be honest, I'd rather write a book than read it. I once discussed this problem with Larry who is my sister's husband and a professional headshrinker. The way he explained it to me is that I'm suffering from an inferiority complex on account of my old man having zillions of books around the house and reading like a maniac. Could be—but I'm not worrying about it. I sort of feel that living life is better than reading about it in books.

I always like to get out for a real long swimming binge before I eat my sandwiches, so that Sunday I put on a pair of fins that belonged to Billy who is a deep-sea-diving enthusiast. Billy comes down to the beach with more stuff than Cousteau took to inspect the *Silent World*: tattered overalls, faceplates, oxygen masks, barbed spears with a line on them, old tire tubes, and other spooky equipment. Billy's a great expert on inspecting the lower depths of Rancho Malibu and a cunning killer of perch, bass, octopus, and abalone. Once he plucked a lobster weighing ten pounds.

Personally, I don't care for all this underwater crap but I do get a kick out of putting on the fins and a faceplate and observing the love life of the abalone—which is quite fascinating, believe me—and that's exactly what I did on that fabulous Fourth of July day.

The coast was flat and even when I started out there was hardly a ripple in sight. I headed out for the wide open spaces which is a cinch with those fins—if they fit over your feet.

A diver can kick a couple of times and smack! he's fifty feet underwater. Besides, you can streak through the choppiest waves with them like a bitchen rocket ship. Little did I know that day what I was in for.

I was out there for about ten minutes slipping in and out the waves, diving down to look around occasionally in some corridors of kelp, coming up for some drags of air again, when this huge thing came from nowhere. A wave as big as a house rose suddenly out of the smooth surface feathering with foam on the top and crashed down at me. Boy, it sure knocked me silly.

When I came up again—and just in time to get a fresh drag— another one came, big and green and swelling, sucking up all the water in front of me. I dove quickly the way I had learned and let it pass, and came up again. Only now I noticed that I was far out—almost at the end of the pier. The place I had started from was nowhere in sight and one tremendous wave after another came rolling in toward the shoal water. The tide was coming in and I was caught in it!

Boy, it nearly choked me. I'd never get back. I realized that I had been swept toward the cove side of the beach. The waves broke here and rolled like a long, incredibly powerful cylinder toward the shore.

I dove, came up again, saw another sky-high wave zooming toward me, dove again, came up—caught air—and screamed.

While I screamed I realized that it was stupid, the noise of the crashing wave almost blasting my eardrums. Who would hear me? Even under the surface it was gurgling and churning by now and green and red specks danced up and down before my eyes.

Once more I made a lunge toward the surface, stuck my head out and opened my mouth to suck for fresh air.

That's when I saw them.

Half a dozen boys squatting barely a hundred feet away from me on their surfboards . . . waiting for the big hump. It was such a funny sight, like a goddamn *fata Morgana*. I wasn't alone anymore. I would be saved.

Again I screamed. No one heard me. Another wave came pounding along. I ducked it. By now the saltwater was biting my eyes. I began to struggle blindly, trying desperately to get to the surface again. I mechanically treaded with my fins, rose up, fought for air—and was all of a sudden lifted to the surface. A pair of powerful arms were around my neck, almost strangling me.

The next moment I felt some hard board under my body and struggled out of the grip that held me.

"Hey, you're choking me!"

"Want a lift?"

I was sitting on a surfboard in the clear water beyond the surfline and the guy who had fished me out of the water had a grin on his face as wide as Joe E. Brown's. I was glad I was saved, but I sure didn't care for that smile on his face. He felt pretty big.

"Hey, Shorty, what're you doing out here?"

He griped me.

"What do you think I'm doing," I said, "looking for some seagull eggs?"

He laughed. "Find any?"

"Sure," I retorted, "I've tucked them under my fins."

That smug grin got smugger—if that was possible.

"Ahhh—that's why you got lost, Pinky." He looked down at my fins as if they were a couple of toilet seats.

"What's wrong with it?"

"What's right with it?" he said dryly.

Damnit, I felt like spitting in his face.

Meanwhile the other guys on the boards came to life.

"Olé, Moondoggie!" someone yelled.

Moondoggie! Some name!

"Who's that fine-looking coozie?" hollered another one. He wore a straw hat as big as a cartwheel.

"Is she for real, Moondoggie?" another surfer called over.

My lifesaver screwed up his face.

"Bite the rag, you guys," he snorted. Then he turned around—I was dangling at the tail end of the board—and said evenly, "Okay, to the nose, Pinky!"

I hadn't the faintest notion what he meant. All I knew was that he had a lousy personality.

"It so happens my name isn't Pinky," I said.

"Getting mad, little girl?"

"Will you please take me to the shore," I said haughtily.

"You hear this, men?" he hollered. "She wants to go to the shore."

"My folks will be worried," I said. "I've been out here for some time."

"Okay, kiddo," said the character they called Moondoggie. "Slide on your tummy up front. I'll get you back to Mamaville."

He sure was playing the hotshot.

I didn't say anything and just did as he told me. He, too, slid down, turned his head to look back toward the onrushing waves, dropped his hands into the water and began to paddle.

I began to paddle with my arms the way I saw the others doing it . . . then a big wave came moving in with a rush. I could feel the water fall underneath me as it rose. It was a smooth and pure wave, not a trace of foam in it. Moondoggie and I tandemed forward with a couple of strokes and the board began to move ahead. I could feel the board being lifted upward as we cut the water with our hands. The speed increased. I got a tremendous kick out of it. "Watch out, Pinky!" he yelled.

The wave was now at its highest peak. For a moment I had this earsplitting buzz in my head, and then—zoom—we went down, the board almost dropped away under our stomachs, the water hissed and roared, foam tossed over my shoulder. Then the noise died down and the board chittered and came to a crunching halt in a few inches of water.

We were in the cove.

I looked around. Only two other guys had made it. The others had got the axe.

I felt so jazzed up about this ride I could have yelled. Moondoggie swung his long legs around and dragged the board ashore. He was tall, I could see it now, all of his gorgeous six-foot-two. "Well, Pinky," he said, "how was that for a pull-out?"

"Great," I said.

"Anytime."

He went down and lifted the board up, swung the thirty-five pounds over his head as if it were a pair of skis and walked away. I stood there like a dope, with those crummy fins still on my feet.

"Hey," I yelled after him, "thanks for the ride."

He didn't even turn his head. A real freep if you ask me. He wore tight blue jeans that had those phony fringes but he had a damn good build I must admit.

About two hundred feet inland stood this old Quonset hut

made from bamboo sticks and palmettos and odd pieces of drift-wood. There was a crude fence built around it, and in the enclo-sure some of the surfers were squatting in the sand, their knees drawn under their bodies. When Moondoggie came up to the fence they called out.

"Hey, Jeff. Some coozie?"

"It's me—and I'm in love again." Someone started on a uke.

"Sharp, real sharp!"

"Ah, blow yourself!" was all my lifesaver said. He wasn't mad or anything. Jeff Moondoggie. Funny name. I yanked the fins off my feet and started back toward the bay where my par-ents sat. I figured they must have had a dozen hemorrhages by now, with me gone for an hour and all. I was impatient to get back to them—but not *too* impatient. I was thinking of the ride on that board with Jeff and I was terribly proud of myself. I wondered whether I would be able to lift that board the way he did and carry it up the beach over my head. Boy, to be able to ride this—all by yourself!

Boards were nothing new to me. I've been skiing for years and I've done some waterskiing too. But this was different. I don't want to sound corny but my heart went flippity-flop and I got all hot inside just thinking of it.

Then I saw this grubby-looking guy with these pants that looked like male frenchies working away with a wood plane on an unfinished surfboard. He had a regular workshop made up on the beach and a sign said WANT BOARDS—ASK STINKY. A few boards—one with a nude girl à la Monroe painted on it—leaned against the fence.

I forgot about my old lady and old man and all and watched the guy. The shavings were flying around as he planed away like a madman.

"Hi," I said.

He said "Hi" too but gave me a big freeze otherwise—just polishing away on that damn board. I wondered whether all surfers were like him and Moondoggie—snooty bastards.

"Who's Stinky?" I asked.

"Me," he said . . . just ignoring me.

"How much is such a board?"

That made him look up. He wasn't exactly friendly as he gave me the once-over.

"For yourself?"

"No, for my Aunt Hester," I said, trying to be funny.

"This is seventy-five bucks," Stinky said, not moving a muscle, "but you couldn't handle it, little one."

I was peeved. "Why not?"

"How much you weigh?"

"Ninety-five pounds."

He screwed up his face and shook his head.

"Can't carry it," he said.

"How about a lighter one?"

He scanned around his workshop, dropped the plane, reached for an old beaten-up thing with a lot of notches in it and lifted it up with one hand.

"What about this abortion?"

"Huh?"

"Twenty-five bucks," he said. "Weighs only twenty pounds. A Wili Wili. Lift it!"

I lifted it. It felt like a sack of pebbles. "I'll put some fiberglass on," Stinky said. "Look like new."

"You'll be here tomorrow?" I asked.

"Sure thing."

"Okay, make it look like new. I'll pick it up at ten."

It usually takes me years to make up my mind.

Also, I had exactly three dollars and eighty-five cents to my name.

Further, I knew my old man would raise a horrible stink on account of being a non-swimmer and getting stomach spasms already when I do a little body-surfing.

But I also knew that the most desperate thing I wanted on that fatal day in July was a surfboard of my own.

I had already decided what to call it: *Moondoggie*.

Y'know, it's probably easier to maneuver one of these things in the water.

Photo by Allan Grant/Time Pix

Three

I made the pitch the following morning at breakfast. I gave that rescue story a terrific build-up . . . listening to me you would have thought that a girl going Malibuways without a board was like a parachute-jumper taking off without a parachute. If my old man would chip in with just ten bucks (having already earlier this morning secured a loan of five bucks via telephone from my sister, Ann—quite a feat considering she's a female Jack Benny but doubled with spades), I could buy the jazziest board this side of the great divide.

Now my old man is a pigeon when it comes to promoting dough for a pair of skis, seats to the opera, the latest Fats Domino album, the Hungarian Relief, a new formal, a trip to Mammoth Mountain, but in matters "Moondoggie," I was biting on granite.

It wasn't the money, mind you—he was dead set against the whole caboodle. Listening to him you would think he *knew* everything about the "goddamn surfboard-riding." It was not for girls, to start with ("never seen a girl on those planks!"), and if it was, not for a girl of my weedy build. Hadn't I read the story of this colored boy who was killed just the other day riding in on a surfboard and being smashed against the piling of Malibu pier? "No siree—over my dead body," my old man said, given to horrible clichés on account of being only a naturalized citizen.

My old lady, though normally sticking up for enterprises connected with the great outdoors, was upholding my old man's appraisal of the whole business, so that was that.

I mean it was "that" for them.

Being a veteran of arguments around the breakfast table my instinct told me that it was useless to scratch further. "Okay," I said, "no sweat, please."

The moment I realized that plan one had gone sour I embarked on alternative plan two. I called Larue who is my girl-friend across the street. Larue is one year older than I and in the possession of a genuine driver's licence as well as a jazzed-up Ford vintage 1930. No kidding. She had inherited it from her mother who had driven it for sixteen years. It's a convertible with a new motor in it and beats a Cadillac any day. Some guy had offered her five hundred bucks for it but she had just looked down her nose at him—and she's got quite a long nose. Everything on Larue is long: her nose, her feet, her arms, her teeth, her fingernails, and when she had the mumps, it was the longest mumps on record. I often feel sorry for her. Her love life is defunct—unless you believe my brother-in-law who figures Larue is sublimating with horses. I hope I'm using the right expression. It sounds sort of dirty. What I mean is Larue is absolutely nuts about horses. She works at this crummy stable all the time and rides the horses of the people who board them there. It doesn't cost her a nickel.

Well, I knew I couldn't lure her to go down to Malibu with me, but I hoped I could wheedle the jalopy from her. She's really a good guy, Larue. It took me some time though to persuade her to let me drive it, but I finally got her to come around. I told my old lady that I was going down to the beach with Larue, which somehow surprised her—knowing about Larue's addiction—but she bought it.

So I picked Larue up and dropped her first at the stables and then out Highway 101 with me to that section of the Rancho Malibu I had discovered the previous day.

The coast was flat and even—not a ripple, as they say so tritely. I was plenty tensed up on account of having to face Stinky minus twenty-five bucks, but I had the three-eighty-five with me just in case I could make one of those installment plan deals.

When I came down to the beach old Stinky wasn't there. I asked one of the guys and he said Stinky was in all probability out there with the boys. Meaning beyond the surf-line.

I looked out . . . and there they were. The whole bunch of them, waiting for an occasional hump. Their boards rose and fell smoothly, no action in sight. It was around noon by then, hot as hell, and it smelled of seaweed and iodine and burned charcoal.

I sauntered over to the Quonset hut, stretched out in the sand near the fence. Some of the surfers were lolling around, soaking up vitamin D. There were a lot of sand fleas and they started jumping like mad. Not that I was particularly interested but I looked around to see whether Jeff was there. He wasn't.

A few boards leaned idly against the fence. They had names painted on them like *Fiasco, Nelly Blye, Tally Ho*.

I got up, strolled over, and ran my hand over the glossy surface. I figured that one of the fellows would see me and maybe offer me a board to take out.

Just then the bamboo curtain to the hut was drawn open and this bum came out. What I mean, he wasn't a bum, but then he wasn't exactly the kind of guy that would drive a girl mad with desire either. He was on the oldish side—around the end of the twenties or so. You got the impression that he had just got up or something. Of course all the surfers in this enclosure wore only shorts or Hawaiian-print bathing trunks but this superannuated Huckleberry Finn had on a pair of jeans that were cut off just beneath the knees and looked more like an old rag bleached by the sun. He was a real tall guy with legs of unbelievable length. Jeez, he was tanned. You've never laid your eyes on a tan like that. Like one of those suntan oil ads you see in magazines—only more so. He had a beard growth of at least three days and he stood there and scratched his stubble and had this kind of empty gaze like he was full of booze.

There was something about the way the other guys greeted him that told me he was a real hotshot.

"Hi, Kahoona," said one.

"Bitchen surf coming up, Cass," said another one.

"Big deal last night?"

"You guys making me some coffee?" said the hut-dweller.

Then he saw me.

I had been watching and my hand was still on *Nelly Blye*.

He came over to me in a shambling gait.

I smiled—and believe me—I practically dislocated my neck just looking up at him.

"Hi," he said.

"Hi," I answered. "That's a neat board."

"Yes, Angel," he said. "*Nelly Blye* is a fine piece of balsa." He was real nice and polite and not condescending like Moondoggie or Stinky.

"I wish I could take it out," I said hopefully.

"You know how to ride?"

"I did it—once," I said. "Yesterday. With—er—Moondoggie." I tried to be real chummy.

A sign of recognition came to his face.

"Yah," he said. "Now I remember. You're the kid Jeff pulled out of the surf. Undine." He chuckled.

Undine? What did he mean? But I didn't care to ask. Instead I said, "What's balsa?"

"That's the wood those boards are made of; light wood. Seven times lighter than cork. But it'll still be too heavy for you."

"I wanted to buy a board from Stinky," I said. "For twenty-five dollars. But I don't have the money."

He rubbed his beard again. Then he turned to one of the fellows squatting in the sand—the one with the huge straw hat.

"I'll take the hot rod out, Pepe. Get some coffee going."

He reached out for the board, turned it sideways, and swung it over his shoulder.

"Come along, kid," he said. "What's your name?"

"It's Franzie," I said. "From Franziska. It's a German name. After my grandmother."

"Mine is Cass," he said, real friendly, "from Cassius. After nobody."

We walked down to the edge of the water.

"You live in that hut?" I asked. I felt real at ease with him.

"For the summer," Cass answered. "Ever hear of a surf-bum?"

"I know some ski-bums," I said.

"It's all the same," Cass replied. "Now you've met a surf-bum, kid."

"I know Warren Miller," I said. He used to be my first ski teacher up in Sun Valley . . . and I remember him telling me how he had once bummed up there for four months, living on eighteen dollars—all the four months.

Ten feet away from there Cass lowered the board carefully and pushed it into the water.

"Be right back, Franzie," he said.

I had hoped he'd take me along, but I was thrilled that he had told me to wait. I watched him as he slid on the board, very smoothly, dug his hands powerfully into the water and headed out toward the surf-line.

I watched him move forward with an even and graceful movement. The waves out there were beginning to form now. Cass got up to his knees, his weight toward the rear of the board. He shot the nose over the foam. When the nose was over the foam he propelled himself forward with a swoosh. He waited for a few moments for a lull, then breezed through the shattered hulk of one wave—and was now in the clear water beyond the surf-line.

The whole operation took no more than three minutes.

Boy, did I get a bang out of watching him.

The waves now started gathering speed. The lazy-looking figures came to life. They turned their heads, trying to figure the steepness of the approaching wave. Then Cass got to his feet— and they all did the same.

If you think you've seen everything when you watched Toni Sailer zooming down the Parsenne or Stein Erikson making the top of Baldy Mountain to Riverrun in Sun Valley in three minutes flat, you're full of bull, kid.

Watching those guys riding in on waves ten feet high, standing up like bitchen lampposts, is something you can't forget for the rest of your life. I guess that's a lousy way of putting it, but when I think back to that first time I saw the Go-Heads of Malibu dragging to shore—that's precisely the way I felt.

Cass was in the lead. They all seemed to follow him. He reminded me of a ballet dancer, tilting the board, cutting across the wave and coming in on a parallel-to-shore run.

A couple of boards somersaulted but the others all came in for a smooth landing. Cass shimmied in just a couple of feet away from where I stood and waited, as if he had figured it out to the inch. He picked up the board in the middle with his left arm and swung it easily over his shoulder.

"Well, kid," he said, "I'm ready for breakfast. Care to join?"

Did I *ever*? I was so proud I could have yodelled.

The other fellows were hitting shore now and I recognized Jeff and he gave me a real goofy look as he saw me walking with Cass toward the hut. Now he put his free arm around my shoulder and I made sure that Jeff saw it. I got a huge charge out of it.

Suddenly Cass asked, "How old are you, Franzie?"

"Seventeen," I said.

Usually I say sixteen but I figured Cass would dust me off right away if I weren't at least seventeen.

"Hmm" he said. "You'll be going to college in the fall?"

"Oregon State," I said. I know a boy I met skiing last winter who went to Oregon State and he had sold me on it.

Cass kept his hand around my shoulder, parked the hot rod and took me right into the enclosure. The other guys looked up in surprise.

He introduced me.

"This is Don Pepe," he said, pointing out the stocky fellow with the huge straw hat.

"Scooterboy Miller—"

"Hot Shot Harrison—"

Some of the other surfers came up now and Cass went right on introducing me. He was a real gentleman.

I met Golden Boy Charlie and Schweppes and Malibu Mac and Lord Gallo and, of course, I needed no introduction to Moondoggie.

The guys weren't exactly overjoyed to have me around. But they showed a healthy respect for Cass.

"Who is *she*, Kahoona?" the guy they called Lord Gallo hollered.

"Franzie," Cass said. "She wants to get the knack of it."

"*That* gidget?" It was Jeff.

Gidget? What's that? The others gave out with a belly laugh. It obviously tickled the trunks off them. I could have spit in

Moondoggie's eyes, right then and there—even though I had not an inkling of what the name meant.

"Let me in on the gag, you guys." I tried to be real cool about it.

The great Kahoona grinned. "It's derived by osmosis," he said. "A small girl. Sort of a midget. A girl midget. A gidget. Get it?"

I got it all right.

Funny, though—the moment they accepted the name they accepted me.

"Okay, Gidget," Malibu Mac said. "Want to go tandem?"

"How about waxing my board?"

"Got any produce?"

"Food," the great Kahoona explained, noticing my puzzled expression.

I had a couple of sandwiches with me, an apple, a banana. In no time flat the guys had demolished the contents of the lunch bag—not a crumb left for me.

Lord Gallo seemed particularly delighted. "Hey—next time bring some more of that stuff," he said. "And how about some booze?"

"Preferably Gallo wine," said Malibu Mac.

"Come along, Franzie," said Cass now. "I'll pour you some coffee."

He pushed aside the bamboo curtain to the Quonset hut, and I followed him.

Inside it was real cozy and snug.

There was not much equipment around—a three-burner cooking stove, a small folding table, a creaky couch job, straw matting on the floor. On the wall—if you can call it a wall—hung a painting. It looked sort of familiar—something with a lot of gay colours. Gauguin, I guess. I saw some of the stuff when I was at that museum in Paris.

Cass poured the coffee in a couple of mugs, flopped down on the couch and said: "Relax, kid."

To tell the truth I didn't feel too relaxed. Something like a cannonball was forming inside my stomach. Also, there suddenly wasn't enough air to breathe.

Through the chinks of the bamboo reeds you could hear the boys hollering.

"Take it slow, Joe!"

"Easy stuff, Kahoona."

"Olé Cradlesnatcher!"

The bongo drums started going.

The great Kahoona just grinned. He took a sip from the coffee and said: "Your ma know you're out here?"

I guess I got dark purple but I managed to say, "I've come to the beach for years."

"There are all kinds of beaches," said Cass. "This happens to be a *special* one."

"I know," I said. "It's for the surfers. I'm just crazy about it. I've got to learn it."

"This is the place for it, all right," said Cass. "But there are also some other things you might learn here. I thought I'd better clue you in. You're a nice kid."

He gave me this funny look.

I sort of guessed what he meant. "I've been around," I said—real mundane. "I can take care of myself."

"You think so?" He squinted his eyes.

There was a pause.

Then he continued: "I'm leveling with you, Franzie. Those guys out there—they're a bunch of roughnecks. Some go to college and all that, but they're bums at heart. Nothing wrong with being a bum—I'm a low-tide bum myself. They're not guys with a fast knife—not killers—but still bums."

"What do *I* care!" I said. "I like them."

The great Kahoona did some more beard scratching. Then he said, "Tell you something, kid. We don't like dames around here. Not while the sun's out. They're always stirring up trouble. Surfing is serious business. Not for dames."

"I'm *not* dames," I said, trying to keep my voice steady.

"You've got the potentialities," said the great Kahoona, and I leaned over. He came very close.

"How old are you, really, kid?"

"I told you—"

"About fifteen?"

The cannonball was back in my tummy only now it felt like a sack of cement.

"I'll be sixteen in a few weeks," I said weakly.

"Don't let it worry you," said the great Kahoona. "You'll get there soon enough."

"*Please* don't tell the others," I said. "I'll die."

The bongo drums were going now like crazy.

Cass reached out and put his big hand over mine. Then he said, "Relax, Gidget. I never told on a pal!"

We got up.

The sun hit us fiercely as we stepped out into the hot sand.

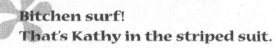

Bitchen surf!
That's Kathy in the striped suit.

Photo copyright © by Warren Miller Photo

Four

Thinking back now I can't tell honestly what got me more jazzed up: the thrill to paddle out on the board and get initiated into the art of surfing—or the fact that those guys made me a member of the crew.

I was "The Gidget" but then they all had their funny names and by the time I could manage a belly slide past the first waves out beyond the surf-line I had forgotten that they had other names and sometimes I forgot even that my name was Franzie and that's no joke.

"Olé—here comes the Gidget!"

"Hey, Gidget, when do we get another leg of lamb?"

"Got some booze, Gidget?"

"Let's drag the Gidget in the hut and teach her some technique."

Boy, I sure felt right at home with the crew. They were regular guys—none of those fumbling high school jerks who tackle a girl like a football dummy. No sweaty hands and struggles on slippery leather seats of hot rods. The bums of Malibu knew how to talk to a girl, how to handle her, make her feel grown up.

Every day—and I managed to come out to the cove almost every day—someone else let me have a board to practice. On Don Pepe's board I learned how to keep in the center and paddle evenly—on Hot Shot Harrison's how to control the direction you're taking with your feet—on Malibu Mac's how to get out of a "boneyard" when you're caught in the middle of a set of breakers—and on Scooterboy Miller's hot rod I learned how to avoid a pearl dive.

The great Kahoona showed me the first time how to get on my knees, to push the shoulders up and slide the body back—to spring to your feet quickly, putting them a foot apart and under you in one motion. That's quite tricky. But then, surf-riding is not playing Monopoly and the more I got the knack of it, the more I was crazy about it and the more I was crazy about it, the harder I worked at it.

Meanwhile home life became one big jigsaw puzzle. First I figured I'd clue my old lady in on the whole operation but Larue talked me out of it. As far as grownups are concerned she wasn't harboring any foolish illusions. "Listen, Jazz-bo," she said, "I know your mom a lot better than you do. She might even let you go out there and wheedle the old man, but you can bet your shaggy fins she's going to mess it up for you. She'll be sitting home worrying and the next thing, she'll be snooping around and she'll be out there in Malibu in the flesh and the next thing, she'll try one of those boards herself and, being the athletic type, she might get a kick out of it and before you know it *she's* going tandem with you and that's the end of the whole blast. Forget it, Jazz-bo, will you?"

Larue's got lots of pimples but she makes up for them with a sound working brain. So I decided to muddle along.

Well, you know how it is when you start with one little old hairy lie—you think you get away with it and then the little old hairy lie becomes one big old hairy lie.

Of course I was telling the truth when I said that I was going out to old Malibu and sometimes one of the girls who picked me up—Mai Mai or Barbara (whenever Larue's car was unavailable)—really came along, but I never took them to the cove, or even near it. They were sort of curious about the surfing crowd, but I managed to keep them at a safe distance. They really had no idea what was coming off—even though Barbara had a couple of fangled chassis that would put Jayne Mansfield to shame.

Then there was the problem of the produce.

You've heard of icebox raids but the way I went gallivanting off with the whole legs of lamb, kegs of cheese, heaps of peanut-butter sandwiches, tons of bananas, was freakishly reckless, to say the least. "Are you feeding the seals?" my mother ventured one day when she caught me surreptitiously stowing away a whole package of wieners in my beach bag.

"Ha-ha." What a laugh. "We're having a wienie roast."

"Who's we?"

"Barbara and I. You know she feeds her tapeworm—and he's nuts about wieners."

My old lady gave me a queer look that spoke volumes. I guess this was the first time she caught on to my horseplay.

However, what I scrounged in the kitchen kept me in good stead with the Go-Heads of Malibu.

Their appetite was monstrous.

They fell over the contents of my beach bag like a pack of hound dogs.

They never had anything edible along and when they got hungry they all chipped in and got some hamburgers over at Johnny Frenchman's joint, and a few bottles of coke and beer. Mostly beer. They could skoal two cases of beer in no time flat. What puzzled me most at the beginning was the great Kahoona. How did he keep himself supplied? There were always some cans of beans standing around in his shack, and coffee and sugar, but it wasn't exactly what you might call a well-balanced diet.

The great Kahoona! I had to think of him all the time. I had seen bums up in the skiing country, like Warren Miller, and then I saw a lot of other ski-bums at Aspen, Colorado, and everywhere my old lady took me in winter. I even once saw a beach-bum in some corny T.V. show with Irene Dunne. He had a shaggy beard *a mile long* and he was always whittling away at some driftwood. But before you knew it he had this beard shaved off and it turned out he wasn't a bum at all but some hack writer who had been disappointed in his love life and stuff.

Well, Cass wasn't that kind of a phony character.

It was Lord Gallo who gave me the scoop one afternoon as I was sitting out in the surf with him waiting for a halfway decent wave to take us in. Lord Gallo's real name is Stan Buckley and he goes to Pomona College and he was the most educated of the guys even though he had this fatal craving for Gallo wine that made him sometimes doddering like a bowling pin undecided whether to stand up or fall down.

"I'll clue you in on that guy, Gidget," said the Lord. "We are all sort of seasonal surf-bums, but Cass is the real article. He's been around from Peru to Nanakali. This here is bathtub stuff for him. Do you know that he's the only guy besides Duke Kahanamoku who came in on Zero break without spilling?"

I had heard about the Duke because Scooterboy had his name on his board and Duke Kahanamoku is to surfing what the Babe is to baseball bugs. But Zero break was Hawaiian to me.

"Zero break comes up only once a year, during storm surf or when there's an earthquake or some ground disturbances undersea," explained the Lord. "Now with all those H-bomb blasts you get them more often. But only in the islands. The waves get up to thirty feet and they come in on a thirty-miles-an-hour speed. Man!"

I was duly impressed. Still, what do you do the rest of the year? I haven't got too good a thinking brain, but right off the elbow I know you've got to have money—*l'argent*—*geld*—and you can't travel around the world on a surfboard.

The way Lord Gallo put it, though, the great Kahoona had made the amazing discovery that you could.

"You may not dig this, Gidget," said the wise man from Pomona, "but for Cass this bumming around the beaches is a way of life ... as the man said. Like another guy goes and sells vacuum cleaners, bumming is his stock in trade. And believe me, it takes as much know-how and talent and brains. He never loses a season on stupid things like trying to make a living or get a job."

"What's he feeding off?" I asked.

"The sea, birdbrain," said his Lordship. "He broils himself some abalone steak or lobster, the kind you can't order at Jack's or King's. Sometimes some buttermouth or perch. Or he scoots up to Pismo for some of those giant clams that you can bake in the ground. Maybe we'll let you come to our next luau, Gnomie . . . then you'll get a taste of it."

Well, that cleared up a few points. It's a monotonous diet, the way I see it, but it can keep a fellow going a long way. I could understand now how much he appreciated my peanut-butter sandwiches for a change.

"The guys are sponsoring him. Ever heard of the great Aga Khan?" he went on. "Well, he's a small operator compared to the great Kahoona."

I ventured one more conventional question: "What's a guy like him going to do when he gets older?"

"He's got a theory on that," confided the Lord among the Go-Heads. "He once told me, 'the only way to get economic independence is to be independent of economics. The more money you make, the less independent you are of it. And once you make a lot of dough, you're more dependent than when you're broke.'"

The Lord concluded his profile of the great Kahoona: "Believe me, Kiddo, this guy's got something. He's found the answer to a lot of things that bother us. The time to start making dough is when you get old and creaky. While you're young, you

got to take a holiday. And he's taken one long hell of a holiday—
ever since he was born."

There were some more questions on my mind like why Cass
had never been married or if he had been, what happened to it,
and also why there was never a girl around the place, and how he
built his shack, and if it was always the same shack, and how he
transported it, and where he went when the season folded in
October, and how it felt when he rode the waves of Makaha at
Zero break, but just then his Lordship had turned his head and
saw a bitchen set of waves coming up fast and he yelled, "Shoot
it!" which means the wave is breaking behind you, and I got in
position and we both missed it and *Fiasco*—that is the Lord's
boat—went into a terrible pearl dive and jackknifed back at us
and we both dove fast and when we came up *Fiasco* was miles
away from us.

And the next thing I know was that some hands grabbed me
and lifted me out of the tide—and if it wasn't again Moondoggie,
giving me this smug, big grin as if he had just been standing by to
fish me out.

I wanted to get off the board and try to help Lord Gallo
retrieve *Fiasco*, but he had a firm grip on me.

"Don't fidget, Gidget."

"Oh, go to Gunneriff!" I told him. It was part of the monkey-
talk I had picked up from the boys. I didn't know exactly what it
meant.

"Take it slow, Joe."

"Turn deaf, Jeff."

That chopped him royal.

Kathy and the crew.

Photo by Allan Grant/Time Pix

Five

I guess the time has come to say a few words about Moondog-gie, alias Jeff Griffin.

Since I know little about the finer technique employed by professional writers in telling a story, I'm probably making a fatal mistake by telegraphing the fact that he was to become one of the principal characters of the ensuing melodrama.

That he had a darn good build I guess I have already mentioned. And he knew it. Boy, if you ever want to meet a guy who was in love with himself I'll introduce you to Geoffrey H. Griffin. He thought he was the sharpest looking guy this side of Baja California. He drove a creamy Corvette with red leather upholstery—one of those rocket jobs that does three hundred miles an hour. The nice thing about it was that he had worked for it the hard way. His old man belongs to one of those pioneer families that stole vast territories of the Spanish grants along the Costa Mare, and wherever they just dug their little fingers into the desert sand some bitchen gushers skyrocketed. But Jeff wanted no part of it, not the winciest little gusher. In fact, he and his old man didn't hit it off too well . . . mainly because Jeff, as I found out, didn't care for the way old Charles Griffin treated Jeff's mother. It's a messy story all around—and Larry, my brother-in-law, would have got a big charge out of it if he had had Jeff on his couch—however, it has little to do with my story.

To come back to his Corvette, he had worked his way through it, you might say, what with having jobs as milkman, mailman, in markets—but most of the money came from working on a road project up in Alaska during the summer of last year. When he came back he entered SaMo City College on account of the lousy grades he had collected in high school. His old man would have gladly sent him to some private college but all Jeff did was flip the bone at his old man which is a very dirty way of telling somebody where to get off.

With the surf-bums at Malibu and points south he felt smack at home. He was happy they made him part of the crew and didn't discriminate against Griffin Oil Corporation. It seems that in the beginning Jeff had to overcome the gang's suspicion that he was just a little snob who wanted to masquerade as a bum for a while, but he convinced them that he could sling the horse manure and shoot the breeze with the best of them. Besides, he had become one of the most affluent sponsors of the big operator.

Which brings me to the subject of explaining what makes a surf-bum a surf-bum. No one in his right mind will be able to figure out how strong and healthy men spend ten to fourteen hours a day in the hot sand or on wet boards, adhering to the adage "Early to bed, early to work is strictly for those who've gone berserk."

To join the fraternity you have to swear on a stack of abalones never to do a day's honest work—at least not while the season is going.

There is something about the hot sand and the relentless exposure to vitamin D that keeps the senses under the continuous spell of a sleeping drug. When Larue asked me one day what in hell I was doing out there day after day (except sponsoring the boys and trying to lick surfing), I sure was at a loss to clue her in.

The state of prolonged anesthesis is of course interrupted once in a while—specially at the publication date of *Playboy* or such pornographic stuff. Someone would sit up and point at some sex display, "Look at those boobs!"

The whole gang came to life.

"Ahhhh—the Ekberg!"

"Some jugs!"

"Phantastico!"

"Are they for real, man?"

"You kidding—they need a hammock for two."

Schweppes, who not only sports a beard but is addicted to poetry, hugged the magazine to his hairy chest.

Do not conceal those breasts of thine,
More snow-white than the Apennine.

Malibu Mac, a regular sex-hound, was the next to give voice.

"Let's drag her down here and give her the time."

"I'll fertilize that Mansfield any day," cried Hot Shot Harrison.

"How about that Lola?"

"Lola—Shmola," said Pepe. "Give me that Sofia Loren. Man, oh man! Some knockers."

There was some dialogue which got pretty rough. I pretended not to listen but got hot and hotter. Bosom talk brings out the worst in me. I'm so self-conscious on account of my meager output and in desperation had turned to some ointment which is supposed to work when you rub it in for three weeks. I did rub and went on rubbing for six weeks but nothing happened.

Well, as I said, I pretended not to listen but lapped up every word of that sexy talk, every single syllable of it. It was the great Kahoona who sounded a note of warning.

"Hey, you guys," Cass said and was casting a glance in my direction, "cut the bull."

"Aw, eat it raw," Scooterboy Miller said, "the Gidge doesn't mind, do you, Gidget?"

"What about?" I sat up . . . putting it on thick.

"Why should she mind?" said Hot Shot Harrison.

"She's a *good* girl."

"I don't know," mused Golden Boy Charlie, "Maybe we're all wet—maybe she's a *nice* girl."

They all looked at me expectantly and, like a dope, I fell for it.

"What's the difference?" I asked.

"Let me explain," said Schweppes. "A *good* girl goes on a date, goes home, goes to bed."

"A *nice* girl," his Lordship continued, "goes on a date, goes to bed, goes home."

"So, what kind of a girl are you, Gidget?" Malibu Mac asked with a leer.

Jeff, who hadn't said a word all this time, came to my rescue. He suddenly got up and came over to me and grabbed my arm. "Come on, Gidget, I'll go tandem with you."

This surprised me to no end. He was the only one who had never taken me out so far—except for the two times when he had fished me from the surf. I was glad he asked me, though, on account of not having to answer those dirty questions. It didn't occur to me then that they were dirty—only afterward.

We went out tandem which is just about the bitchenest thing going. You have nothing to do but to lie on your stomach and paddle out. You're just a passenger on the board. That's what it's called. The guy behind you is called the "steerman." You're supposed to paddle all the time sort of in the same rhythm as the steerman. Like rowing a boat. Then, when you're clear from the break and the board is under control, the steerman gets to his feet and tells you to get up too. If any waves are going, of course. Then the passenger has to lean slightly forward and place one foot ahead of the other for balance. Or the steerman takes you on a bareback ride. This is the most fun and that's what Jeff did with me that afternoon.

I rode in on his back and boy, was it a blast. He must have had a great time himself because he said, "Let's go out again, Gidget." So we went out again and waited for another good hump and when it came he did another "standing island"—meaning he didn't spill and I had my hands around his head and felt just great.

The old heat just pounded down on us. My skin started blistering but we went out again and again because you just can't loll around and shoot the breeze and lie to the sun when a set of waves is going like it did that afternoon.

I forgot what time it was, *where* I was and all, and I forgot that I had promised to be home by five and it was *seven* by that time and my folks had almost six hemorrhages apiece and, besides, I ran a fever of one hundred and three.

They called Phil Rossman and he gave me a shot of something and I practically passed out.

And then that very night, I had this real crazy dream.

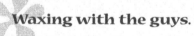

Waxing with the guys.

Photo by Allan Grant/Time Pix

Six

That dream must have been one hell of a production and I must have projected it with all the sound effects going with it, because my ma sat on my bed and she had grabbed me by my shoulders and I heard her yelling at me like she was crazy, "Franzie!! Franzie!!" real frantic. And the next thing my old man came rushing into the room and he had only his pajama top on on account of an old habit and I had to laugh even though I still ran some fabulous temperature.

They both stared at me.

"What's the matter?" I said.

"You had a nightmare," my old lady said.

"Shall I call Phil?" my old man asked. That's the first thing he *always* says. He's some hypochondriac, but as long as he can get Phil Rossman on the phone and talk to him, he thinks he won't die and neither would anyone else in the family. I guess you call this fetishism or something.

My mother, who's much more practical, put her lips to my forehead and then pronounced that my temperature had dropped and told my old man to get back to bed and shot a withering look in the direction of his hairy legs.

No sooner had he staggered out of the room than my ma gave me this funny look and asked, "Did you dream about a dog?"

"Huh?"

"You called for some Moondoggie," my old lady said.

"Oh," I said and didn't remember a thing.

"Who's Moondoggie?"

"It's a boy."

"Hmm," the old lady said—as if she knew everything.

She didn't probe any further, though. I had to swallow a couple of aspirins and then my old lady went back to her room, telling me to call her if I needed anything. Our rooms are across a hallway.

It was a bright night with the moon out in full display and I was lying wide awake now and staring at the ceiling. There's a crack on the ceiling and it looks like a gnu in flight but this night it looked like something else . . . it looked like a surfboard going over a big hump and as I was staring at it all of a sudden I had this goofy sensation I've read about named "total recall."

I remembered what I had dreamed, only it wasn't like a dream at all. It was so real, like the moon that shone or like that gnu in the ceiling, only more so.

I got hot. And then chilled. And then hot again. It had been that kind of a sensation. It must have been what they write about in all the books my ma wants me to read all the time and I never could buckle down to—except for the real sexy passages.

In my dream I had a love affair with Jeff. Only it wasn't what you think. It was *being* in love. Which is probably much better than having an affair. We kissed. And he told me that he was in love with me. I could hear his voice. And he asked me whether I could love him too. And I said, "You're the man I've been waiting for. I love you. I always loved you. Don't leave me. Don't ever. I'll die if you leave me."

We were lying in the sand and telling these crazy things to each other and I think I was even crying a little bit on account of being so lovesick.

I had never said to anybody that I loved him. Except maybe to my old lady when I was a kid or to my sister, Ann, but that was also a long time ago. I certainly haven't said it to a boy ever. Of course in those silly daydreams you have, you imagine being in love, but that's something else again. Once in Berlin when my old man was on his sabbatical I went to this crummy American school and had this terrific crush on John who was a G.I. I almost told him that I loved him. But then he got married to one of those dumpy German fräuleins and I was glad I never told him. He was a real dunce, I found out later—just lonely in Germany on account of being from Iowa, and that's why he walked me home and even took me to the movies a couple of times.

And once in Switzerland I also thought I was in love—he was an American boy too—but then it was because *I* felt lonely and homesick for America and all that, and Chuck was just over there for a skiing trip. I was only fourteen then and I guess at that age it isn't the real thing.

But as I was lying in bed and recalling how it was in my nightmare with Jeff, I suddenly knew that the way he kissed me and I had kissed him, so splendidly, so perfectly, and the way I had cried—that this was how it must be to be in love. Something like bubbles bursting happened to me. I didn't go to sleep anymore that night and when my old lady came into the room I smiled at her and squeezed her hand which made her somewhat confused. When you're in love you love everyone and because I couldn't tell it to Jeff, that I had fallen in love with him, I told my mother that I loved *her* and I didn't feel corny at all.

My mother took my temperature and it was still up in the nineties. So Phil Rossman came again and slipped me another dose of penicillin and looked into my throat and told me that my tonsils looked like a couple of golf balls and told my ma that he had told her a dozen times that they should have come out and stuff. And my old lady gave him the same answer that she always gives him when I have yearly tonsillitis: "Over my dead body!" Meaning *her* dead body.

Phil said I would have to be in bed for a week at least. I smiled at him because even though he is at least forty he is a bitchen-looking guy for a doctor and for a moment he looked like Jeff to me. That was the fever.

Only then it struck me that he had said "a week in bed." My eyelids were burning and my throat got tied.

I wouldn't be able to go out to Malibu for at least ten days! Jesus H. Christ!

"You've got to cure me in a hurry," I told Phil. "Maybe you can give me some stronger stuff."

"What's the matter?" Phil asked. "This is vacation."

My ma said, "I know what's the matter." She gave me the old X-ray treatment and I knew right there and then that she really had me.

No sooner had the medicine man gone than my mother sat down at my bed and had a heart-to-heart talk—meaning she did the talking.

She told me that she had a hunch for the longest time that I was being dishonest about my daily beach excursions with Larue and Mai Mai and Barb. She hadn't said anything because she wanted me to come to her and tell her the truth. "And mothers have instincts," she said. She knew I was fibbing and snitching stuff from the icebox and now she wanted to know who "Moon-doggie" was.

"I'm sorry I didn't tell you," I said. "I was so scared I couldn't go out anymore."

"You've been surfing!"

"I'm learning," I said. "It's the toughest thing going, but I'm learning. The Go-Heads are teaching me."

" 'Go-Heads???' "

"The guys out there," I said. "Don Pepe, and Lord Gallo, and Hot Shot Harrison—and Schweppes. He's got a beard like in the ad in the *New Yorker*. He writes poetry. And the great Kahoona. He's absolutely fab. He's been surfing with the Duke at Makaha."

My ma gave me a real goofy stare. Then she recovered.

"You forgot Moondoggie. You moaned and groaned his name all night."

"That's Jeff," I said, "Jeff Griffin."

"How old is he?"

"Oh, nineteen about."

"And the others?"

"They're all going to college."

"Aren't they too old for you?"

"They think I'm seventeen," I said.

That went over like a lead balloon.

"They're too old for you," my old lady said.

"They're just *right* for me," I said. "I'm a member of the crew. Do you know that I'm the *only* girl they took on? You know what *that* means?"

"It could mean a lot of things," said my ma—real dryly.

"Well, you've got to let me go out there again," I said. "I'm really more grown up than you think."

"You're a baby," my mother said. "Look at you. You haven't got sense enough in your dumb little head to know when to get out of the sun ... or to protect your skin ... or to wear sunglasses—or to tell the truth. Cheating is not being grown up. It's downright adolescent. I have to talk with your father about this. Now take another aspirin."

She left the room.

I felt real miserable then. I fell into thinking that maybe she was right. Maybe I was just *playing* being grown up—the way I always did since I can remember. Putting on my sister's bras and formals when I was only eight, smoking cigarettes, and putting on false eyelashes and talking to some phony Hollywoodville characters, inviting them to cocktail parties. I remembered the date I made with that guy at the travel office in Venice, telling him I was all alone in Italy on a trip around the world. Of course, I guess it's the normal thing to want to jump a few years ahead when you're fifteen, but maybe my jumps were real *salto mortales*. It occurred to me that ever since I came back from Europe

I had become especially desperate to grow up. Any minute I felt it would happen. Not biologically, I mean . . . that's long behind me. But emotionally and all. I would be out of school, out of the home, just out. And I would have a man, of course. We would go around the world together; we would see all those jazzy places I saw with my folks—Italy and all that. That man I imagined had no real face, like one of those skin divers having their faces covered by a mask, but I dreamed big Technicolor productions, and some so embarrassing if I typed them my ribbon would turn pink.

As I was lying full of penicillin that morning those daydreams came visiting me, only with the difference that now the skin diver had taken off his glass plate and I could recognize his face. That face became suddenly the answer to everything I had been waiting for all my life: "I have to tell him," I said to myself. "He doesn't know yet, but I must tell him." If I'd had the phone in my room and if I'd known his number, I would have called him right then and there. I couldn't stand it, I thought. Ten days to be away from him. God, how I loved him! How wonderful it was to be kissed by him.

I closed my eyes and tried to redream the scene, but it didn't work. But because I felt so full and smothered with love and I couldn't tell anybody, I got a paper and pen and wrote a letter to Jeff—a long and passionate letter in which I told him about the dream and how I felt about him and that I had found the love of my life. Ten pages, spiked with the most embarrassing details. And while I wrote I became so emotional that my eyes became charged with hot tears.

It was terrific.

Then I reread the letter and found it almost worthy of being printed in an anthology.

I felt utterly exhausted after I was through with writing. I rang the bell for my old lady because I was parched. But before she came in I tore up the letter and put the scraps under my pillow.

Kathy and her dad, talking in the study.

Photo by Allan Grant/Time Pix

Seven

That lousy tonsillitis kept me in bed one whole week. It was the longest shortest week in my whole life. Long because I couldn't stand being away from Jeff, and short because he was with me all the time. We had the most gruelling love affair since Paul and Virginie with only one slight hitch—namely, he wasn't with me. Well, I was floating nevertheless. I read Françoise Sagan's *A Certain Smile* three times. I never could figure why Dominique left Bertrand for old Luce. Imagine letting a doll like Bertrand go to waste on account of an ancient lush like Luce. While I simply goofed off seeing myself in a French bed in Cannes, I had Fats Domino warbling "You know I love you, yes I do, and I'm saving all my lovin' just for you."

I even tried starting to write this story, but I didn't get very far owing to the fact that it was only the beginning, meaning the best was yet to come.

The second day out of bed I was ready to tackle old Malibu again. Secretly I had started to use the bosom rub once more and even though I had lost a couple of pounds in other parts of my anatomy, I was thrilled when I saw myself naked in the door mirror. The rub had taken.

I had all but forgotten the little worm in the apple, my parents. Funny—they seemed to have adjusted to the facts of life. Not once during the week was Malibu mentioned. It should have deepened my suspicion but it didn't. I'm so gullible, it's not funny.

The sinister note in the proceedings crept up in the person of my brother-in-law, Larry. He dropped in sort of casually the second day I was out of bed and had just started reading *From Here to Eternity* for the sixth time (meaning the dirty passages). He asked me to go to lunch with him.

That was strange. He's a busy fellow, as I mentioned before, being an analyst guy and shrinking people's heads with the help of a single couch. His special concern is little kids. If they still wet their pants at the age of four or set fire to their younger brothers' or sisters' playpens, or if they bite their governesses' butts, parents who can afford it send them to Lawrence H. Cooper, M.D. His office is right in Beverly Hills and, believe me, he has the greatest racket going. For twenty-five bucks an hour those little tykes are brought to his office and play around with toys and dolls and stuff. All Larry does is sit around and watch them. Honest. And scribble down his private observations. It's really something. Those little beasts are "acting out" their repressed feelings—that's what it's called. They give dolls the names of their little brothers and sisters, for instance, and stick needles in their eyes or throw them against the wall or bury them. It's good therapy. Larry writes it all down and then explains to those little monsters what they are doing and *why*

they are doing it. It needs a great deal of patience all right. Sometimes those kids start hitting the therapist (I guess grown-ups get
that urge, too, but can't act it out), but when they do they have to
leave. Still, the parents are charged the full hour. Some deal.

But I'm digressing again.

Well, I'm quite fond of Larry. He's the typical "gray flannel
suit" sort of fellow—crew-cut, pipe and everything. Dapper. I
thought it was real nice of him to come by and take me out for
lunch—being the gullible type as indicated. He said that Ann
wanted to come along but that Becky, who is my two-year-old
niece, had suddenly developed a tummy ache so she had to stay
with her.

We drove in his black T-Bird to Frascati's, which is right on
Wilshire Boulevard and very continental with red-checked table-
cloths and all and the food is really *in-time*—if you go for that
kind of stuff. Also the waitresses are all from France or Belgium
and I spoke to them in French but they answered in English.

We had a good time, shooting the breeze and Larry telling me
about this one little girl patient of his who flushed the doll she
named after her father down the toilet. The father was a T.V.
producer.

After lunch Larry offered me a cigarette which struck me as
rather peculiar but I took it. He asked me whether I smoked a
great deal and I told him that I had a weed once in a while—especially when I'm out Malibuways with the crew.

"The crew?"

"The gang out in Malibu. Don't tell me you haven't heard
that I've taken up surfing?"

"Not the faintest idea," the liar said.

A phony if I've ever heard one. I had told Ann a lot about the guys and I know that she and Larry discuss me continuously.

"Tell me something about it," Larry now said, offering me another cigarette. "Is it fun?"

This was the second cigarette. I took it. And then it hit me. All of a sudden. Boy, how could I have fallen for a gag like that? Taking me out to Frascati's and playing the gasser and offering me a cigarette. *Two* cigarettes. The whole thing was as flimsy as a cobweb. Well, I decided then and there to give that sleuthing headshrinker and my doting family a dose of their own medicine.

"*Is it fun!!*" I underlined every syllable, giving him a confidential smirk.

I could see on his face that he thought he had me. He threw all professional caution to the wind.

"Come on, tell me," he said, "about the crew—"

"They're the greatest bunch you've ever met."

"Oh, how come?"

"Because they're grown-up men," I said, "not freeps like the boys at Franklin High."

"Freeps??"

"It's a cross between a freak and a creep."

"Haha," he laughed, real hammy. "But aren't they more your speed—the—er—freeps?"

"*My* speed? Where are you living, Larry? In nod land?"

"Huh?"

"Have you been sleeping?"

"Oh," he said dumbly. "I hardly think so. Don't forget I'm dealing with kids all day long."

"And you think I'm still a kid?"

"I sure hope so," Larry said.

"Well," I said, and took a deep drag from the cigarette, "let me clue you in on something, I'm not."

He got a shade paler.

"You mean because you're going out to the beach and hanging around with these beach-bums?"

"I thought you didn't have the faintest idea?"

"Now wait a moment—you just told me—"

"That they are a great bunch. Not *bums*."

I always knew he was the lousiest psychologist going.

"Listen, kid," he said, "I've seen those guys . . . you can't tell me."

All of a sudden he had *seen* them.

"You say the same things like Ma and Dad," I said, "and I always thought you're not a square."

"You call a fellow a square just because he calls a bum a bum?"

"They're the greatest guys you've ever met."

"You've said that before."

"They can stand it twice."

"This is all so—er—general," Larry said, "I wish you'd be a little more specific."

M-hm, he was getting closer.

"You mean," I said, giving him a mysterious smile, "you want to know who that greatest guy is?"

"It sure would help."

"So you can go back and squeal on me?"

"Would I?"

"Why not? You're part of the family."

"And is there something the family should not know?"

I didn't answer that one. I just sat there and smiled and blew some perfect smoke rings against the blue sky.

Larry H. Cooper was squirming in his seat.

"Listen, Franzie," he said, "I'm a doctor. Don't forget that. Whatever you tell me is strictly a professional secret."

I had him on the hook, bleeding.

"There is nothing to tell."

"Who's this—er—great guy?"

"You *really* want to know?"

"Of course."

"His name is Jeff," I said. "Jeff Griffin. His old man has zillions of oil wells."

The color came back into Larry's cheeks.

"Oh," he said, "then he's not one of the . . . bums?"

"He's an honorary bum," I said.

"And what makes him so different from the boys who date you?"

"For one thing, he's older. Nineteen. He goes to college. And he was in Alaska . . . and in Europe . . . and in Japan too."

I was really flying high.

"That doesn't necessarily make him a great guy."

"It does—in my book. He knows how to handle girls. He has finesse. No sweaty hands, no making out in drive-in movies."

"Making out??"

"My God, Larry, where've you been living. I guess you still call it necking."

"Oh, I see. And you kids—er—don't neck?"

"*I* don't," I said with dignity.

"Well, then you and this boy, Jeff, you're just pals?"

"Pals??" I smiled. The torrid love scenes of my feverish night flashed through my mind. And something else too.

"Oh—er—has it gone a little further?" Larry asked.

"A *little*??"

His mouth sagged.

"Keep on trying," I said. I got a great charge out of it.

"I guess he's just like any other college boy then," Larry said, still hopeful. "Trying to find out how far a girl like you would go."

There was a pause. Then I said sort of matter-of-fact: "If a girl goes all the way, a boy doesn't have to find out."

Poor Larry. He almost toppled off the chair. The edges of his mouth began to pucker. He looked sick.

After he had swallowed hard a couple of times the disciple of Freud and Rorschach said, "Really, Franzie, I had no idea—"

"Well, *now* you have," I said, killing the cigarette.

"Check!" he called.

He paid with slightly shaky hands.

We walked together over to his office which is just around the corner of Frascati's.

We didn't talk but I could sense the old brain behind the crew cut clicking at top speed.

When we got to the entrance of the medical building I stopped.

"Well, I guess I'll take the bus home. You're probably busy. Thanks for the nice luncheon."

"You come up with me," said Larry. "I must talk with you."

"We just talked," I said.

"I mean *seriously*."

"You gave me your promise—"

He was quite unnerved. "Well, I don't know whether I can keep that promise."

"Aha," I said, playing surprised.

"I'll keep the professional secret," Larry stammered, "but I have an obligation to the family. They—"

He stopped . . . and *I* finished the sentence: "They sent you after me, didn't they? They told you, 'Why don't you have a talk with the kid? Find out what's going on there in Malibu with these bums. We don't know what to do about it. It's not the right crowd for her and it's dangerous. She's nuts about this boy, too. He's probably a hoodlum like the rest of them. She doesn't tell us, but she might tell you. You have a better approach; you're a psychologist. Maybe she needs some therapy or such. Find out and then tell us.'"

The sickliest smile appeared on his face.

I couldn't keep a straight face any longer. I had to laugh.

"Okay, Doctor," I said. "*Now* you can tell them!"

He just stood there and shook his head.

"You fed me the bull," he finally said.

"You've been asking for it."

"Well—I'll be damned!"

Boy, was he relieved. I was still laughing and now Larry started laughing too and soon we were both laughing like a couple of hysterical jackasses.

And this would have gone on for some time if we hadn't suddenly caught sight of a little boy of six who stood there with his colored maid and stared at us.

As it turned out, he was one of Larry's patients, just on his way to the office for a little session in child-therapy.

He was quite a cute little kid and he looked up at the maid and said: "Let's knock off, Betty. The Doc's gone schizzy!"

Gidget-mania.

Photo by Ernest Lenart

Eight

The next day, a gorgeous August day, found me tooling down the main drag toward the familiar haunt.

Larry's relief over my well-preserved virginity was so fierce that he had called my old man the very afternoon of our luncheon and sold him a double size of Freud and Adler, well mixed. I managed to be on the extension phone in the house while he talked to Dad in the study—which is a little annex attached to our house.

"Listen, Paul," he said, "I had a good long talk with Franzie and I guess I have it all figured out. It's quite harmless, believe me, and just the normal pattern. She wants to be free from control, and she wants to show her independence. All this dirty language and smoking cigarettes and putting on mascara are just the obvious signs of juvenile rebellion. The best way to get her over it is to give her all the freedom she wants with certain limitations. If she's so dead set on the surfing crowd, let her go out and surf. She's not going to take any chances—on surfing, that is. She feels at home there. It bolsters her self-confidence. Good social adjustment, if you know what I mean."

"I haven't got the faintest idea what you mean," I heard my old man grumble. "I want to know about this doll."

"Seems a nice kid. Good family."

"Some kid! He's nineteen. And I hear those boys out there do a lot of funny things—drinking, smoking, and God knows what else."

"You mean sex, Paul?"

"Damn right, sex!" my old man said. "And Franzie is snoopy as a cat in that department. Maybe just because she's not quite developed for her age."

"It's normal to be curious, Paul."

"Save the bromide, Doctor," said my old man with an edge to his voice. "It's one thing to be curious and another to be obsessed by it."

"Who's obsessed?" I heard Larry chuckle.

"Americans!" my old man bellowed. "I just read what Sorokin at Harvard said the other day. And he's an authority on human behavior. Wait a second . . . I'll read it to you."

The line went dead for a few seconds. My old man was looking for the paper. He gets all heated up when it comes to the subject of sex.

"Listen"—he was back on the phone—"'Americans are victims of a sex mania as malignant as cancer and as socially menacing as communism.' Hear that?"

"I hear," Larry said, "but what does it mean?"

"It means," my irate father went on, "that 'our civilization has become so preoccupied with sex that it oozes from all pores of American life.' That's what it means. And I'm quoting Sorokin. Sex has become—"

Just then my old lady came through the door and I had to put the receiver down. Darn it, just when it got really interesting.

I worried all afternoon but strangely enough at the dinner table everything was supremely serene. I didn't even have to challenge them. They gave me their official permission to tool out to the beach, not their blessings mind you, just permission. But I had to promise to be home every afternoon by four— bitchen surf or no bitchen surf.

So I was on my way again, richly stocked with produce for the boys and anticipating a royal welcome.

Besides, I was all jazzed up with the things that were happening inside me. The dream—that gorgeous dream—I had relived and relived it again and again. It had almost become reality. Maybe, I figured, it had happened to Jeff, too. And if it hadn't, I was all prepared to tell it to him.

I had gone over the dialogue for days, and I had laid out the action. I would ask him to go on a walk with me down the beach and we would lie down in the hot sand and I would give him a long, long, look and then I would say: "I dreamed of you, Jeff. I kissed you. And you kissed me. It was heaven. And now it will become reality. I want to be close to you. Very close. I love you, Jeff, I loved you from the first moment I saw you."

I would have puked if I had heard these lines on the movie screen, but when I said them they sounded like the most unique and luminous words ever exchanged between a man and woman.

I parked the car on the highway and, loaded down with food and beach bag, I made my way toward the hut.

Don Pepe and Hot Shot Harrison were lolling around. The others were all out there beyond the surf-line, waiting for the humps.

"Hiya, kid," said Hot Shot Harrison . . . lazily.

"*Saludos,*" waved Don Pepe.

That was all. Not one word about my lengthy absence.

It sure took me down a few notches. I offered the guys some of the cookies I had made and, as usual, they whaled them down like greedy sharks.

I asked Don Pepe to let me have his board and, slightly deflated, I headed out.

Well, the crew was all there, even the great Kahoona, and he called out, "Hi, Gidget!" But that was the extent of the royal welcome I had anticipated. Then I spotted Jeff and I maneuvered the board over to him.

"Olé, Gidge," he said. He was smoking a cigarette. "Lousy surf."

I knew right then that he couldn't possibly have dreamed about me. Yes, I doubted if he ever would.

"What's new with the crew?" I said. My heart was beating furiously.

"Not a damn thing."

"You had good surfing?"

"Pushing a lot of green water."

"All week long?"

"I went down to San Onofre over the weekend with a couple of guys. We had some giant wetbacks."

"That must have been a blast."

"Oh, yeah, it was out. Sunday night we had a great booming party. I came home at six A.M."

I gave him a big grin. But the words froze in my mouth like a waterfall at sub-zero.

A gentle set of waves came rolling in and began to steepen. I tried to get to my knees, but they felt wobbly, like molasses. Then I slid on my tummy and made it to shore with the others coming in on standing islands.

I dragged the board back to the hut and the others came in too, cursing the crummy surf and then falling over the produce in customary fashion. Not a word of thanks for the lush tollhouse cookies I had baked. But the thing that really got me was that not one, not one single one, asked me where I had been.

For a moment I became choked and aching with disappointment. Then I suddenly realized that I was no member of the crew—simply a blind passenger. If I had never come back no one would have noticed it.

I was overcome with self-pity and desperation. How could I have kidded myself all the time? I wasn't in their league. I was half-sized—a gidget. I'd never make it like Jeff or the Kahoona, standing on that board and come riding in a standing island. I'll be sixteen in a few weeks, but I'll never grow up. I'll always be pint-sized, cute perhaps, but never like all the other girls, popular and wanted by boys and whistled after. I will love but no one will ever love me back. Not Jeff. I won't be able to make him love me. I won't be able to help myself. I hate it. I won't.

I got up quickly. I felt the tears starting in my eyes and I walked away, down the beach to a spot where no one could see me and when I got there I flopped down and threw myself into the hot sand and let go, and my heart was trembling and quaking, and the tears were wetting the wet sand, and then the fit had passed and I dried my face and sat up again and looked out over the quiet ocean, and soon I felt calm again. I've heard of kids getting those kind of emotional jags, but it was the first time I had to go through it. To tell the truth, it felt real good.

And then something extraordinary happened. Maybe you think it wasn't extraordinary, but it was something big to me. I saw Jeff coming down the beach, looking around.

He could have been looking only for me.

I got so excited, like some bongo drums going inside me. He came over and flopped down into the sand—very close.

"What gives, Gidget?" he said. "Feel like being alone?"

He said it kind of awkwardly.

It would have been the moment to say it. All that wonderful monologue I had rehearsed. He was so close beside me that I could have touched him by merely moving my hand a few inches.

Instead of looking into his eyes I stared straight ahead of me and heard myself saying: "I often feel like being alone—thinking."

"Oh," he said. "What about?"

"All kinds of things."

"You haven't been around for a while," he said. He didn't ask, but I could feel he was curious. Why hadn't he said it before, I wondered.

Now I looked at him with a slightly mocking, mysterious smile.

"Well," he said, "you don't have to tell me if you don't feel like it."

Suddenly I had this crazy idea. It wasn't a very original idea—I had read about it in *A Certain Smile*. In the book she was only seventeen, Dominique. But couldn't it have happened to *me*? I certainly had *felt* like her. And I had been away for ten days. Like Dominique in the South of France with tired old Luce. It would certainly sound better than having been in bed with tonsillitis. The Côte d'Azur was sort of far away, but the Côte d'Monterrey had its points too.

"I was up in Carmel," I said, still with a faraway gaze.

Funny—as I said it I saw myself in Carmel. I even had a dead ringer for old Luce—Dan Anderson, a friend of my old man who lives up in Carmel right on the seventeen-mile drive. We had stayed there once for a week and he's a sweet old guy, something around forty. I couldn't see a girl of seventeen going wild over him, but over a distance of four hundred miles he served his purpose.

"With your folks?" Jeff said, slightly bored.

"I sometimes take trips all alone," I said.

"You were *alone* up north?"

"Alone," I said.

I was lying down, crossing my hands under my neck, and closing my eyes. I had heard that slight change in Jeff's voice when he had asked whether I had been alone. If my technique had worked with a sharp guy like Larry, it would work with Moondoggie.

He must have moved closer, for all of a sudden I could feel his hand touching my shoulder. I didn't move though.

"Is there—er—some surfing up at Carmel?"

What a silly question. He knew darn well there wasn't.

"I really had no time to look around for surfing," I said. I again permitted myself an enigmatical smile.

"Well, what *have* you been doing?"

It was the first personal question he had ever asked me. It was also the first time he didn't call me Gidget.

"Why don't you ask me who I was there with?" I said. I opened my eyes. The sky was white, shimmering with heat.

"I really don't care," he said.

"Of course, why should you?"

He picked up some pebbles and threw them aimlessly toward the dunes.

"Tell me, Jeff," I heard myself saying, "you *do* think I'm a little girl, don't you?"

"Yeah, I guess so."

"Why?"

"You're so damn dense and all," he said.

"If you only knew—"

"For instance?"

"I've been around, Jeff. I've been traveling. I was in Paris and Rome and Venice . . . and on the Riviera."

"Sure," he said and laughed—sort of condescendingly, "and in Carmel."

He kept coming back to it.

"I'm really much more mature than you think," I said.

"Oh, sure."

"Lots of men think so. Dan, for instance."

"Dan who?"

"Up at Carmel."

"The guy you've been visiting?"

"M-hm."

"Who's he anyhow?"

"A writer."

"A *writer*. For Christsake! Probably one of those faggots that hang around this place. Carmel is full of 'em."

I hadn't the faintest idea what a faggot was. Whatever it was, the Dan I knew wasn't it.

I smiled wisely. "Dan is no faggot."

"Then what *is* he? What does he write?"

"Books," I said. "He got a prize once. I mean, he's really famous."

"He must be pretty old then," Jeff said. I seemed to detect a scant note of relief in his voice.

"He's around forty," I said.

"Well, so what do you do with a guy of forty all alone?"

I didn't say anything. I just permitted myself a delicious sigh. There was one paragraph about Dominique's experiences that I had read over and over again, because I visualized myself in the very same situation—not with old Luce, to be sure. "He caressed me," it read, "and I kissed his neck, his body, everything I could touch of his shadow profiled against the nocturnal sky. Then I lost sight of him and the sky as well. I was dying. I was surely going to die, but I didn't die, I only fainted. How could anyone fail to remember this forever?"

"You haven't told me," Jeff said.

I looked way, way out into the Pacific where the sky ripped into the blue water.

Then I quoted Sagan, only it didn't sound like a quote: "How could anyone fail to remember this forever?"

Boy, did *he* give me a look.

"Is that a line out of this guy's books?" he said eventually.

I could see he wasn't up on modern French literature.

"You're such a baby," I said. I reached out and gave his cheek a little pat. It was meant to be real casual, but my heart leaped inside me up into my ears or whatever it is your heart leaps to.

He was really confused now.

Then he got his swagger back and stood up. "Okay, let's go back."

The temptation was terrific but I stuck it out.

"You run along, Jeff. *I'd* like to stay a while longer, thinking."

He gave me another goofy look and moseyed along.

"See you later, alligator."

I watched him as he slowly walked back toward the cove. Had he bought that story? Why did I do it? Why didn't I say it the way I meant to? "I love you," I whispered after him. "Forgive me, Jeff. Love me back, please . . . love me back." I was all jumbled up.

I followed him with my eyes all the way to the bend of the dunes.

Then I jumped up, raced down to the edge of the water, and threw myself into the onrushing waves.

Teenagers and telephones. Need we say more? That's Dad in the background.

Nine

The phone was ringing that very evening while we sat around the dinner table.

I usually get the jump on it, but I had just finished a one-hour-straight marathon talk with Larue and felt instinctively the bell wasn't tolling for me.

Brother, instincts!

My old man returned to the table and said, "I wish those callers would at least have the courtesy to give their names."

"For me?" I leaped to my feet. "Male or female?"

"If it's female, it's a ventriloquist," said my old man. Some joker.

In the hallway I grabbed the receiver.

"Who is it?"

"Hi," said a voice.

Jesus H. Christ! It couldn't be! Phone in hand I made a dash for the hall closet and bolted the door.

"How did you get my number?"

"There is something like a phone book," Jeff said.

"But, you don't even know my name."

"There is something like a beach bag."

"Have you been snooping?"

"Relax, kid," he said. "What're you doing tonight?"

"Tonight? Nothing," I said, a bit too quick.

"Good deal," said Jeff, "I'll pick you up."

"You have my address?"

"Sharp as a marble," Jeff said.

"Wait a moment," I said, "I've got to—" I caught myself. I couldn't possibly mention my parents. After the bull I had fed him on the beach.

"You got to what?"

"What do you want to do?"

"Ah, not much. Take a little spin. Maybe look into the Sip'n Surf."

"Okay," I said, "half an hour."

"I'll be honking," he said, and hung up.

Half an hour. My thoughts were racing in ten different directions. Got to change. Got to swipe Ma's high-heel shoes. Got to swipe Femme. Sexy red sweater. Feed the old man some bull. My hands felt like they'd been dipped into a bucket of ice.

I scrammed out of the closet, but on the way back to the dinner table I managed to switch to a pose of detachment that was anything but calm.

I even sat down again to finish my dessert.

For a moment nothing was heard but the thoughtful intake of green Jell-o.

Then my old man asked: "Who was the doll?"

"Geoffrey," I said.

"Geoffrey who?"

"Griffin. One of the crew. He asked me over to this girl's house. They're showing some surfing movies. I'll be back by ten."

"You look at night at this crap you do all day long?" He was casting a jaundiced eye at my mother.

"If she's back by ten—" said my ma. She's okay when it comes to tipping the scale.

My old man frowned, but didn't pursue the argument.

I raced into my room and got dressed with zero break speed. I spilled some of my ma's Femme, and the whole room reeked like a coozie's boudoir.

Jeff was right on the dot and I streaked along the corridor towards the exit leaving behind me a heavy cloud of Marcel Rochas, when my old man blocked my way.

"Wait a moment, young lady. I want to meet this dreamboat if you don't mind."

"I'm late," I cried frantically.

"Your father is right," my mother said. "Bring him in." You could see she, too, was curious as hell.

My mind works fast in a crisis. Maybe it was better to bring him in now than have my old man lurking in the dark when he brought me home. He'd done that a couple of times with other boys and it had embarrassed the hell out of me.

"Okay," I said, taking a wild chance. "I'll ask him to come in . . . but just for a minute. And *please*, Daddy, don't give him the old X ray treatment. He's not a freak. He goes to college."

It was just water off a duck's back.

"Let's see that doll," was all my old man had to say.

I dashed out.

When Jeff saw me coming down the driveway he jumped out of his Corvette and opened the door for me. Boy, did he look dapper. Up to now I had seen him only in his bikini. He wore a light-gray sweater and his face had the color of cork.

"Hi," I said, real debonair. The way he looked at me I could tell my appearance had made a dent.

I stepped into the car and as he leaped into the driver's seat I suddenly said, "Oh, crum, I forgot my bag."

Quickly I stepped out again and then, just like an after-thought, I turned to him. "Say, why don't you come in a moment? I'm sure my folks want to say hello. They've sort of old-fashioned ideas."

He didn't seem exactly wild to follow me.

"Please!" I said.

He lifted himself out of the car and trailed after me with marked reluctance.

I made the introduction.

My mother said, "So nice meeting you," but my old man just stared at him like he was a geek out of a sideshow.

"Would you care to come in?" my mother said.

There was an embarrassed silence.

"Gee, Ma," I said, "some other time. We've got to see that picture."

"Yah," said Jeff quickly, "we've got to be going. Some other time."

There was another exchange of frozen grins and we were on our way.

"Take it slow," my old man called after us. Wouldn't he! It burns me the way he always inserts his corny two-cent platitudes.

The whole thing went so fast that Jeff didn't even notice that I had stuffed my bag into the side pocket of the car.

It wasn't quite dark yet, but the sun was halfway down.

"What picture do we want to see?" Jeff asked.

"Oh, I just had to tell them *something*. You know the questions they can ask. To them I'm always a . . . baby."

"Yah," he said. "They can be trying. I dusted mine off a long time ago."

"Don't you live with your family?"

"You kidding? I live in a fraternity."

I quickly looked for his fraternity pin. In an upsurge of foolish ecstasy I saw the pin already on my red sweater. It was nowhere in evidence.

Jeff turned the radio on, but it wasn't a hit parade song. It was some classical music. I didn't mind. I leaned back and looked up at the stars and listened to the music and when the piece was finished the announcer said we had heard a master recording of the "Fair Maid of Perth." I guess I'll never forget that tune to the day I die.

I had no idea where he was taking me. I didn't care. If he would have proposed elopement and would have driven me right down to San Diego and on over the border to Mexico, I wouldn't have minded. I felt so idiotically happy and gone that I didn't notice how tense Jeff was. Only later did I remember that his hand was clammy when he helped me out of the car at the Sip'n Surf down in Santa Monica Canyon.

"Let's just take a look," he said.

The place was empty. A crummy bar with only one lonely sot perching over the counter.

"Hiya, Charlie!" Jeff waved at the bartender. "How's the boy?"

"The boy's great," said Charlie. "And how's the bad dad?"

"The bad dad's sad," said Jeff.

It must have been a running gag between the two.

"Couple of beers," Jeff ordered.

Charlie gave me a puzzled look even though I had applied a good shot of eye-shadow and wore my old lady's highest heels.

"It's okay, Charlie." Jeff gave Charlie a wink, wide as the prairie.

"Do you come here often?" I asked.

"Once in a while," he said, "with the crew."

Charlie brought two beers and I skoaled with Jeff. The beer tasted like hell, but I would have swallowed it if it had been rat poison.

After this Jeff seemed a little more relaxed. He went over to the jukebox and inserted a coin. Some soft purple music came from the loudspeaker and Jeff took me by the hand. "How about it?"

We danced. The light was dim and there was some stale tobacco smell in the air, but it didn't seem to matter. I was almost perfectly happy, in a dazed, numb way. I wanted nothing but to be in his arms and go on dancing forever. I grew an octave higher as I clung to him. He was a fabulous dancer.

When it was over I just looked at him. We hadn't spoken one

word. He understood me. He inserted another nickel and we danced the same melody and it was even better then.

Then some guys came into the bar, and Jeff got nervous suddenly and said: "Let's go on driving, Gidget."

We went back into the car and it felt like coming back to your home.

"Listen," I said, "do you know I happen to have a name?"

"Sure." He grinned. "Gidget."

"I was born Franzie," I said.

"Let's keep it Gidget," Jeff said.

We drove down towards Malibu and when we came to the "Rock" Jeff turned off the pavement and stopped the car facing the ocean.

He put his arms around my shoulder and he drew me close to him. He turned my head and there was barely light enough in the shadows to see how he was slightly trembling around the mouth just before he kissed me.

I had been kissed before but never like this. It was like in the dream only now it was for real. Fire flashed to my fingers, to my toes. I was burning. "I love you, Jeff," I whispered.

Funny, he didn't say a thing. Not like in the dream when he said he loved me, too. Frankly, he didn't seem to care when I told him. It seemed to bother him. He sat a moment in silence and looked out into the water. It's hard to talk to someone you've just kissed . . . and horrible to sit silent. Jeff must have felt the same way because suddenly he said: "Let's go down to the beach."

"Do you think we should?"

"Why not?"

"It might be damp down there." I got scared.

"Don't be afraid."

"I'm *not*."

"All right then."

He helped me out of the car and I pressed my arm against him and we scrambled down the steep incline that led to the dunes.

We sat down in the sand and it wasn't damp at all. It was a real balmy evening. There were some fires burning along the coastline and the fires were reflected in the ocean.

"Look," I said, "the waves all lit up. Spooky, isn't it?"

He nodded, kind of absently. Then he grasped at my shoulders and pulled me down to the sand with him.

Again he kissed me, but it wasn't as good as the first time in the car. Maybe I was too scared or he was too frantic. It felt like he wanted to prove something to himself or as if he were trying to see how far I would let it go . . . how gettable I was.

I struggled and freed myself.

"Please," I said. "Let's not lose our heads."

My God, a line right out of *True Confessions*!

Jeff let go of me. He gave me a funny look, then reached for a cigarette and lit it. He didn't offer me one.

All of a sudden I felt like crying. I wanted to put my cheek against his and tell him that I loved him and that this was all I wanted. I wanted to tell him that I was only fifteen and that all the love affair I ever had was with him, Jeff, and that one only in my dream. I wanted to tell him to love me just a little bit and have patience and we would love each other forever.

Jeff didn't say much and I didn't know how to spark up the

conversation. Everything seemed suddenly dead. Maybe he was thinking of the story I had told him, about Dan and Carmel, and he probably figured it was all one big rank phony.

He got up. "Okay, Gidget," he said, "let's get moving." He helped me up and we started back to the car. It seemed so unfinished. Why didn't he talk?

When we got back into the car I sat very close to him, but I felt a tension in the air. It wasn't the way it ought to be. Even the sea was deserted now, blue-black with only some fire sparks here and there.

We didn't speak to each other until we reached the house. All the way I tried to find the right words I wanted to tell him and just as he brought the car to a stop I turned to him and said, "I guess you probably know, Jeff, but I told you a big fib. I tried to show off. I haven't been up at Carmel. I was in bed with tonsillitis. What I told you this morning was only a line out of a book. You were right. But please, please don't be mad at me. I thought it'd impress you." I fought my tears. "It's just because I had this . . . this silly dream about us."

"Us??" He turned to me and screwed up his face in sarcastic disbelief.

"Don't you dream sometimes?" I said.

"Oh," he said. "*Those* kind of dreams."

He laughed.

"Don't," I said. "This was really serious."

"So it was. And what am I supposed to do about it? Apologize?"

"You don't have to do anything about it," I said. "I only wanted to tell you."

"Okay," Jeff said, "forget it. I knew that hot story you dished up was not so hot. But I don't care." He paused and then he took my head into his hands and lifted it up to him. He kissed me. He kissed me full and hard and real long. I had never known kissing was like that.

"Oh, Jeff," I whispered, "you're not mad at me?"

"Did it feel like being mad?"

"I love you," I said.

"Please," Jeff said, and backed away.

"Don't you want me to?"

"No," he said. Then he added quickly, "You can kiss me though. I like the way you kiss."

"And you don't want me to love you?"

"Do I have to spell it out?"

"But why not? Don't you like me?"

"Yes and no."

"Why 'no'?"

"You're too young for it, Gidget."

There it was again. It takes so long to get old. I wished I could have grown up over night.

"I'm getting older every day," I said. "It's the way you feel inside that counts."

"The crew would think I've gone in for cradle-snatching."

"Is that what's worrying you?"

"They'll kid the pants off me."

"You don't have to tell them," I said. Too quickly I said it. I was willing to compromise just to be near him.

The moment I said it I knew how clumsy I was.

"I was afraid you were getting funny ideas," Jeff said, "and I don't want that. If you dream, it's your own responsibility. But don't think I've been just sitting around waiting for you to come along."

For a moment I sat in frozen silence.

Then I said, "Who is it?"

"Don't be so nosy, kid. I don't owe you any explanation."

"Is she older than I am?"

"Eighteen."

"Blond?"

"Brunette—and tall."

"Thanks for telling me," I said. I bit my lip.

"I guess I had to tell you. Want to call the whole thing off?"

I was stalling for time.

"Where is she?"

"Up north, for the summer."

At least she wasn't *here*. When you're in love you make adjustments fast.

"Has she got your fraternity pin?"

"Listen," he said, "I can show you her picture if you're curious."

"Chop it," I said.

For a moment I wondered whether I would die before I got into the house, into my room, into my bed. The dream. Would I dream again?

Suddenly it hit me. Did I really care whether he had another girl? Whether he was going steady with her or whether she was tall or hip or square? Didn't I always see me as the heroine in a tragically beautiful melodrama? Now I wouldn't have to act grown up and sophisticated, and I could go on loving him and wouldn't have to do the things that I didn't understand and that frightened me.

Boy, can you sell yourself a bill of goods if you're gone on a guy!

"Well," I finally said, breaking the long silence, "at least you've been honest, not sneaky and underhanded as I was." I even managed a smile.

Jeff smiled back. He seemed relieved.

"Glad I haven't hurt your feelings, Gidget."

"You haven't."

"I had a nice time."

"So did I."

I opened the door. Before I got out, I put my arms around Jeff and kissed him long and real seductively. I got a terrific charge out of it, thinking of that dark brunette up north.

She may be wearing his pin, I figured, but look who's kissing him now.

Bathing Queen.

Photo by Ernest Lenart

Ten

If you want to know what goes on in Loveville you've got to live there. I took up permanent quarters and I dug it fast. Dig Number one: being gone on a boy is more important than having a boy gone on you. Dig Number two: you have no compunctions whatsoever and you could do *anything* to be close to him. Close . . . and as soon and as often as you possibly can manage. Dig Number three: *ad infinitum*.

In other words, you simply can't stay away.

It's a shattering experience but I guess the sooner you learn it the better for you.

"Listen, darling," my darling mother said, "are you by any chance *chasing* this boy?"

"Whatever gives you this idea?"

"I don't have to read tea leaves, Franzie. But you're making a horrible mistake. A boy's got to chase you. It's as old as the mountains."

"You talk about your European mountains," I said. "The ones here are different."

"You can't wriggle your way out with wisecracks," my wise mother said. "I have eyes—and ears."

"Have you been *listening*?"

"How can I help it? First you groan in your sleep and now you moan on the telephone. Now if Jeff wants to pick you up you don't have to talk him to shreds to come by."

I knew how right she was. But how can you help it? As stated above: you can't stay away.

So I kept calling him.

First thing in the morning and last thing at night.

And don't think he didn't resent it.

He resented it, but he talked to me for hours on end. What did we talk about? Well, mostly how I felt about him, and he, mostly how he didn't feel about me. His conscience was torn by remorse and he always brought up Stella in his conversation— Stella who was up north and the possessor of his fraternity pin . . . and who wrote long letters, letters he tried to read to me but I refused to listen to.

I had promised to treat him no differently from the gang in Malibu, but love has a super way of advertising itself and they were sharp guys. They smelled that I was having it bad.

Especially the great Kahoona. He looked down at me from his lofty six foot four with eyes full of wisdom and compassion as if to say, "I wish I could help you, angel, but if you love you've got to suffer. There's just no way around it."

I suffered. Don't think I didn't. But it was a real cherry, delicious way of suffering. Jeff belonged to another girl. She had the cake, but I had the frosting.

I stubbornly refused to accept the fact that she was even alive and the only question I once asked was whether she could surf.

"She's been out here once watching me," said Jeff, "but she wouldn't get on a board come hell or low tide."

"Then you're badly mated," I ventured.

"Listen, Gidget," he said with a big smirk, "there are other things than surf-riding, praise the Lord."

"Are there? Well, you can eat them raw," I shot back.

I knew what he meant and why he rubbed it in and in my anger and frustration I added: "I bet there are zillions that can do what she can—but not many girls can stand up on a board."

"It'll take you two more seasons, Gidge," he said. "Maybe three."

"Two more weeks—want to bet?"

"Two weeks! Ha! You slay me, kid. You have the imagination of a half-ripe turnip."

"Bite it," I said, and headed for the surf-line.

I would practice with a maddening frenzy whenever the waves were going and I was able to snatch a board from one of the sponsors. No more tandem . . . I had to go it alone. Some mornings I was the only living thing out there, working like a fiend to lick some giant wetbacks. Ten, fifteen times I worked my way out through the waves, trying to come in a standing island and each time the axe fell on me and chopped me into the breakwaters.

Toward the end of the day Jeff and I would sneak away from the hut. First I would leave and he would follow ten minutes later.

There is a small cove all but hidden from the highway, with two huge rocks standing guard. This was our meeting place. There we fought and shouted and fell into sudden silences. And there we kissed each other and I felt his warm, sun-heated body. Strangely though, his kisses became more gentle, more sweet and it didn't feel like he was regretting kissing me. But not once, not one single time, did he tell me that he loved me.

Some days we would just sit there and watch the sun going down, and even though he didn't say what I wanted him to say so badly, I felt this was how it is between two people if they're in love because not the words that are spoken are the ones that count, but the ones that you never speak—except maybe to yourself.

 **Awkward!**

Photo by Allan Grant/Time Pix

Eleven

And now I embark on that portion of my story which I promised myself to put down in my most elegant English. It has real drama and contains that very important element labeled by teacher Glicksberg as the "clincher" or climax.

But, before the final curtain rises, let me record a little incident without which there would be no third act.

That incident occurred in the middle of the last week in August just a few days before the "Giant Fiesta," also called the "Big Luau"—an event that had been looming ominously during the second part of the month—"ominously" because it was the biggest shindig or conclave of surfers and I would have given one of my canines to be invited, but I hadn't been.

I had sent out feelers for quite some time but all I heard from the crew was, "Cram it, Gidget, this is nothing for you" ... "Sure, there'll be girls around, but not good girls like you, Gidge" ... "We don't want the law barging in on us, Gnomie. Ever heard of the Mann Act?"

I tried, of course, to enlist Jeff as a fellow conspirator but he was the most violent Holy Joe of the bunch. He almost yelled his head off. "Have you gone crazy!? Those guys bring all their coozies along. Ever heard of an orgy? You haven't, Gidget, but this is an orgy. So just chuck it."

How could I? The very word. Orgy! I had to look it up in my old man's *Funk & Wagnall*'s . . . and it is listed there as "a wild or wanton revelry." It goes way back to Pythagoras who directed his disciples in some secret rites to practice gymnastics, dancing, and music.

Well, that didn't sound so debased. I found it downright treacherous of the crew to unload me on an event like this, considering how much I had sponsored their inner men all summer long. I got all blewed, stewed, and tattooed, but that's how far I got. I remained the uninvited.

And then this screwy thing happened, just as I was about to throw in the sponge.

We were squatting around the hut that afternoon after a full day of bitchen surfing when Don Pepe came rushing down the steep little hill leading from the highway. The crew had dispatched him to Johnny Frenchman's for a case of beer and while the guys were parched and all ready to skoal the case, there didn't seem to be any reason for Don Pepe to come flying down like a jackrabbit chased by a rattlesnake.

"Hey, Kahoona," he panted, "there's someone up there looking for you." He jerked his thumb in the general direction of Highway 101. "A dame," he added.

He didn't have to spell it out. We all saw it. It was a dame all right.

She was languorous and she had a scarf around her dark hair and she carried—of all things—a parasol. The parasol she used for the descent to the dunes. Besides that dainty red parasol the visitor was equipped with the highest heel shoes ever to touch the sands of Malibu. No wonder she had a hell of a time to negotiate the two hundred feet from the highway to the hut.

I got all excited not knowing what was coming off, but sensed real drama. Some of the guys sat up and watched the visitor's approach with leering anticipation. The only one who looked like he wholeheartedly wished to be a hundred fathoms beneath the Pacific with a couple of sandbags tied to his feet was the great Kahoona.

The most vapid expression I had ever seen on a man whitened his face. His desire to bolt was so acute that he even made a couple of abortive steps in the direction of the waves. Then he stopped. He looked frantically around and his eyes caught sight of me. Besides the approaching visitor there was no other female in sight.

"Come along—quick," the great Kahoona hissed ... and practically dragged me by the hair into the hut. Then he turned back once more and yanked my beach bag with contents after me. I looked dazed. For a moment I felt as if I had stumbled by mistake into an Alfred Hitchcock picture, except there were no cameras around to film us. Cass emptied the contents of my bag—a spare bathing suit and the Merry Widow that goes with the spare, on account of that lousy bias-cut uplift arrangement—and hung them like a shop window display over one of the folding chairs. Then he whispered: "You got to help me out, Franzie. Just lie down there on the couch and pretend you live here with me."

A real movie plot. I was right. For one delicious moment I could emote in a real-life drama and quickly I decided to play that bit to the hilt. I reached for a cigarette the way I had seen some broads reaching for it in numerous movies and draped myself on the creaky couch in a fashion worthy of Marilyn Monroe. I remember I even slipped off the shoulder straps of my bathing suit and gave my bosom a hefty push upwards. The scant light filtering through the bamboo sticks into the hut helped the impersonation considerably. The great Kahoona lit the fire and started the coffeepot—playing house.

From the outside came a lot of whooping and hollering and some appreciative whistles. And I heard Schweppes say, "*Mister Who?* Never heard of him. If you're looking for the Kahoona you'll find them in there."

And presently, swinging her hips with dignity, the visiting dame stepped into the hut.

Coming from the stinging light of an August afternoon she seemed at first to be blinded. She didn't see me. But she saw Cass. And she said simply—and I guess you'd call it throatily, "Hello, Cassius!"

The great Kahoona gave a brilliant imitation of a man caught with his pants down.

"Buff. Why—how—I mean how did you get here?"

"I've looked up all the deadbeats from Coronado to San Onofre," said the woman called Buff. "That's where I got the tip-off."

The great Kahoona went over to her—and he behaved most genial, "Great to see you, Buff. Really great."

She just stood there silently and stared at him and then she stretched her arms out and any second she would have thrown herself on his bare chest had I not quickly emitted a discreet cough.

Buff froze in a silly gesture of outstretched hands. "Somebody here?" she asked with a dead voice.

"Oh, yeah," murmured the great Kahoona, and he added sort of dumbly, "haven't you seen her?"

Now she saw me. Her mouth opened like a goldfish and it stayed open for a long moment.

"This is Franzie," said the great Kahoona with an elegant gesture towards me. It was all so idiotically phony—I decked out on the cot in a bathing suit, the white-faced Buff with high heels and red parasol ogling me, and the great Kahoona in his bikini acting as if he were impersonating an impeccably dressed David Niven in an English drawing-room comedy.

Lying down you don't look so dwarfish and, besides, it was rather dark. Miss Buff kept staring at me and I smiled up at her, not saying a darn word. All her jealous female instincts were tingling— you could almost *hear* them tingling. And with an anger, cold like moonlight on a winter's night, she said to Cass, "I wanted to talk to you *alone*." She underlined alone by repeating it a couple of times.

For a split second I deliberated whether to vamoose but I watched Cass for a clue and the clue didn't come. Instead he said, "Fine, Buff, let's walk down to the beach."

"Walk??"

It sounded as if he had suggested to her to jump from the pier with her red parasol opened up.

"Well, I'm afraid we can't talk very well in here," said Cass, pointing at me and—gruesomely corny—at the Merry Widow hanging over the chair.

"Helpless rage" was another cliché that had sprung to my mind as I searched the face of the languorous Miss Buff. Another moment of pregnant silence and then she said, "All right, let's walk."

It became evident to me that all Cass wanted was to get her out of the intimacy of his four bamboo walls. And with my help he had succeeded.

Buff turned and without batting another of her long eyelashes at me, dissolved into the glaring sunlight of Malibu beach. I guess before following her, Cass threw a grateful wink at me, but I'm not sure.

I had played a short bit in this melodrama lying there mute in the half-dark like one of Madame Tussaud's wax works. I held the unlighted cigarette still between my fingers.

Now I lit it and stepped outside.

Cass and his visitor had sauntered off in the general direction of the Colony and the two sure looked like a picture created by Salvador Dali—especially Miss Buff in her high heels trying to lick the quicksand by using the parasol as a crutch.

Instantly I became the center of the crew's breathless curiosity.

"Wha' happened?"

"Who's the chick?"

"She's an unknown around here!"

"Tell us, Gidge!"

"He's got it made in the shade with *her*."

"She must be one of the winter recruits."

They were curious as hell, but so was I. And all the positive information we got came from Don Pepe who had spotted her on the highway and reported that she had arrived in a slick English sportscar.

Jeff came over to me and I could see that he resented the way Cass had used me for a patsy.

"Did he try to pass you off as his coozie?" he grunted.

"So what? I'm glad I could help him out."

"Probably one of the former Missuses?"

"Has he been married?"

"I bet he *has* been. He's not flit."

"Flit?"

"Stands for faggot."

"I see," I said, still not having the faintest idea what a faggot stands for.

Speculation ran high and a couple of boys even laid bets that the big operator would fold up his tent and go the way of all flesh, but I told them it was all too obvious that he had tried to dust her off and that if my instincts were right, Miss Buff would be out with a snuff.

They all liked to hear me say it. In a roundabout way they all were jealous of anybody—male or female—who entered the hallowed orbit of the great Kahoona.

Well, it couldn't have been more than an hour when the couple appeared again on the horizon. An instant hush fell over us. They walked by the hut without giving us a look. You could see that they were really wrapped up in something.

When they came to the little trail leading to the highway, Cass took her arm and was helping her up to the plateau, real gentlemanlike.

It couldn't have been more than five minutes and we saw him

coming back to the hut. Nobody said a word. We just sat there and waited for Cass to say something, but he didn't—not one word. All he did was pick up one of the boards (it was Lord Gallo's) and he went down to the water. But before he went he turned to me and said: "Thanks, kid, I'm much obliged."

Obliged. That was the cue I'd been waiting for. It wasn't too ethical but I decided right then and there to ask him for something in return. So I waited till he came riding in and then I jumped up and dashed down to catch up with him.

"Cass," I said, "how about Saturday?"

"How about what, kid?"

"The luau—am I invited?"

"Well—are you?"

"It's up to you," I said. "Is she coming, Buff?"

"She won't be back," Cass said.

"Then I *did* help you," I cut in quickly. "I was old enough to pose as your mistress—that should make me grown up enough to come to a lousy beach party."

He smiled. I had him there. He hoisted his board as if it were a sack of feathers and walked toward the hut. I went right with him.

"Listen, kid," he finally said, "I'm not extending any formal invitation. But why don't you just drop in? I'm not going to boot you out, pal, if that's what you're scared of."

Well, it wasn't exactly the way I hoped it would be, but when you're desperate you sort of reach for the proverbial straw.

And I *was* desperate about that party. Don't ask me why. I guess somewhere I felt that no matter what speed your imagination works, if you're not asked to the big luau you just can't call yourself a regular member of the crew.

The shack on the beach. Cozy!
Photo courtesy of Kathy Kohner Zuckerman

Twelve

On the outset everything worked in my favor.

I had mapped the most devious plan to dupe my family since old Stonewall Jackson chopped Pope royal at Bull Run, but the plan was not set in motion. On Friday, quite suddenly, my parents decided to go up to Lake Arrowhead with some friends. Naturally they wanted me along. And naturally I told them that, much to my dismay, I couldn't come along. There was this Tri-Y party at Mai Mai's which I couldn't possibly miss.

Boy, what a gigantic order for horse manure.

I hadn't attended a Tri-Y meeting for ages. If you want to know why, those wholesome squares in my club bore the living hell out of me with their crummy meetings—and I'm using the sentence advisedly, avoiding a word much closer associated to horse manure. All they do at these meetings is to yak-yak about *other* Tri-Y clubs, about their laughable amatory exploits, consisting mainly of some Senior saying "Hi" to them in the school corridor, and comparing the monthly expansion of their chests.

They're real babies, believe me. They haven't got the foggiest notion what's coming off.

History bears witness that the biggest lies go over with a bang and that bull about the Tri-Y meeting was no exception. Imagine, I would be able to stay out Saturday night as long as I wanted— no one there to control me! It was one of those creepy coincidences which happen in life, but when you write them down they sound so colossal phony.

Well, Saturday came rolling around and my folks departed and I was on my own. I had decided to contribute to the crew's inner man by baking a "Strietzel" in which I'm an expert, having watched my old lady do it every Christmas. It's a delicacy of my ma's native Austria and actually nothing else but a coffeecake laid out in braids, with plenty of nuts and raisins baked into it. I spent four hours of the morning in our kitchen and had even employed the assistance of Larue, but what finally emerged from the oven didn't resemble anything Mother used to make. It was a real abortion and certainly unfit to boast with at a beachcombers' fiesta. So Larue and I dug into it and tried to pass the rest off to our two cats, Hexl and Naftl, but even they refused to be hoodwinked. So the rest was committed to the incinerator.

Around noontime Jeff called.

Larue answered the phone and said it was the maid speaking, the way I had instructed her. She also said that I wasn't in and wouldn't come home before evening.

How childish can you get! Well, as childish as a girl going on sixteen. And that was barely three months ago. And did I grow up! Overnight as the saying goes and in my case, the old cliché certainly ran true to the old cliché.

The reason I didn't go to the phone then was as follows: I didn't want to lie to Jeff about the evening. Had I told him that I would come down to the party he would have popped a blood vessel and we would have got in a long and hairy fight and in the end I would have probably resigned. And the farthest thing from my mind that Saturday was resignation.

Further, I wanted to surprise him.

He called a couple more times that afternoon and both times I heard his voice, but hung up.

Larue helped me get dressed. I have this real cute Mexican flary skirt and I put it over the bathing suit and as a top I wore just a simple white blouse with a very low cut. My bosom looked real firm in it, I must admit.

I could hardly wait till seven. I had Larue's jalopy and I started my wheels in the direction of Malibu.

I was excited as a cork about to pop from a bottle of champagne. What would they say? How would I behave? How would Jeff take it?

It was one of the hottest evenings of the summer. Never had I seen the sea bluer, the sand more golden, the hills more purple— or do you say purpler?

As I tooled along the highway completely wrapped up in my orgiastic fantasies, I heard the tooting of a car horn. Actually I didn't hear it at first, only when the car was alongside me and the honking got so earsplitting that it almost created a traffic snarl. If it wasn't Jeff in his Corvette buzzing me like an angry traffic cop!

I flashed a reckless smile at him, but what I saw flashed back at me was something else again. We were heading for the same destination, but we were also heading for disaster. "T. S.," I murmured—and you have to figure for yourself what the initials stand for.

We parked at the old stand on Highway 101 and parked alongside us was the most motley assembly of vehicles ever to disgrace a U.S. highway. You could have had a pick from all shapes and forms of beat-up jalopies to funeral and delivery trucks converted into trailers. Jeff had parked behind me and he now came up to me and I could almost *hear* his blood boil.

"And where do you think you're going," he said, as if he didn't know exactly where.

"If you'll calm down for two seconds, I'll tell you."

"Who invited you?" he said, still in top gear.

"Aren't you glad to see me?" I said.

"Please go home," he said, quietly.

"Cass said I should come," I said. "I belong here. And what's it to you anyhow—unless you have invited some coozie?"

"You don't even know what it means," said Jeff. "This is an all-night affair. You're out of place, Gidget."

"I still have time to go home. Come on. Don't act like a square."

"Do your folks know where you went?"

"You don't need to worry—they're out of town."

I linked my arm in Jeff's. He wore a pair of blue jeans and a white sweatshirt. We kind of fitted right together. I felt real sensual, just touching him. He backed away.

"I don't know what you want to prove, Gidget," he said, "but as far as I'm concerned you can count me out for tonight. *I* haven't invited you to the party."

And he turned and scooted off and let me just stand there, holding my beach bag.

My poise went to shreds, right then and there. I had been convinced that Jeff could be wheedled, but as it turned out I was the lousiest wheedler going.

Oh, what's the use, I told myself, and was ready to turn around and drive home again when some hand grabbed me. It was Lord Gallo.

"How," he muttered . . . and he was swaggering slightly.

In his free hand he was swinging a gallon bottle of his favorite beverage.

"You look great, baby," he said. "Come on, let me carry you."

And without further ado he gave me the firemen's lift. He hoisted me on his shoulders and carried me down the trail toward the hut.

"Look what I found up there," he announced and sat me down right in the middle of the circle of the crew.

Boy, did they yell and scream and break out in war whoops.

"The Gidget! That tears it, the Gidget is with us!"

A huge fire was going and suspended over it hung a black kettle. The great Kahoona stood over the kettle with a ladle and tasted the chowder he had brewed from sand crabs, sea mussels and rock oysters.

I was overwhelmed by their spontaneous enthusiasm over my appearance only to find out that they were too far gone to care one way or the other. They had already annihilated kegs of beer and started to get fractured on Gallo wine. I saw a lot of guys I had never set eyes on before and they were decked out in what was unquestionably the screwiest collection of rags ever assembled anywhere.

And then there were the coozies.

If you want to know the truth, I hadn't had the faintest notion what a coozie looked like . . . except that they always called them coozies and that it made me curious, naturally. Now the coozies assembled around the fire that evening were really nothing to write home about. They were girls of eighteen or twenty and they were a swell bunch—except that they didn't look like they had much outdoor activity. They were laden with an enormous quantity of costume jewelry and their hair had gone through all the shadings of the dyeing process. From their brand-new bathing suits you gathered that they had not been overly exposed to the outdoors. Some wore just shorts and those fuzzy little sweaters where you could see right down to the navel, and there was one they called Adele who had on nothing. I mean she had one of those French jobs on where you just cover the most delicate points of your anatomy. Another one had a bathing suit made from leopard's skin and she had slunk herself around Hot Shot Harrison like a leopard even though I wouldn't know how a leopard slinks itself.

No one bothered to introduce me to the newcomers so I just got up and took off my skirt and blouse and went for a quick dunking in the surf. It was still pretty hot even though the sun was down and a creepy wind was blowing. It was one of those icky desert winds we call the Santa Ana, the one that streams in from the valley beyond the mountains, ventures out into the Pacific, doing a cute whirl, and returns to shore.

I did some bodysurfing and the rest of the fellows who were still out for the last ride came in with me just as it got real dark.

When I got back to the fire, they offered me some of that vile-tasting bouillabaisse and Don Pepe fixed me an abalone sandwich which tasted like my old man's huarache fried in deep fat. I had to get this horrible taste out of my mouth so I drank a can of beer and because my tongue felt like a large, dry sausage, I drank another can. After this my stomach felt as if the bottom were coming out so I had to go into the hut and lie down for a while.

All this time I looked for Jeff, but to be sure, Jeff hadn't looked for me. In fact, he made elaborate efforts to let me know that, as far as he was concerned, I was not present. He had planted himself firmly into the sand with some of these lousy fish dishes and a case of beer. In the fashion of a beachcomber for-saken in some African jungle, he got himself all boozed with alcohol and self-pity. The only thing that made me feel good about this childish sulking of Moondoggie's was the fact that he had come alone to the luau. No coozie had planted herself on his stomach.

As I was lying there and contemplating the fickleness of the male psyche, Cass entered the hut. He struck a match and lighted a hurricane lamp hanging from the ceiling. He looked so damn handsome that evening wearing a pair of tight-fitting Levis and a faded red T-shirt. He came over to me and sat down on the cot.

He put his square, tanned hand beneath my chin and turned my face upward.

"How do you feel, kid?" he asked.

"Little woozie—I had a couple of beers."

"That's a couple too many."

"I'll be okay in a jiffy."

I couldn't very well tell him it was his lousy chowder that made me sick.

He looked at me real friendly and all of a sudden I wondered what it would be like kissing the great Kahoona. I guess it wasn't a sexy thought at all, though I admit a lot of my thoughts drift in that direction.

Outside a phonograph started playing "Baby, if I made you mad, something I might have said—"

"We better join the crew," Cass said after a pause. "The guys might be getting ideas."

"Who would?"

"Jeff, for instance."

He gave me another searching look.

"He doesn't give a hoot."

"He does," said the great Kahoona, "besides giving you a rough time."

Jeez. How did he know?

As I pointed out, they're sharp guys and the great operator obviously operated with four eyes—two at the back of his head.

"He didn't want me to come here," I said. "Now he's sulking."

"That's a favorable sign," said the great Kahoona, and smiled his wise smile. "I wouldn't be surprised seeing him charge in here like a mad bull if we'd only stay a couple of minutes longer."

"I can't figure it," I heard myself saying. "He's got a steady girlfriend. Why does he care whether I get drunk or passionate—or drop dead?"

"He probably can't figure it out himself," said Cass. "That's why he's getting loaded."

It was a profound bit of philosophy and coming from the big operator himself, I was properly impressed.

The racket outside grew wilder. I stood up and while I still felt wobbly, I managed to leave the hut with the Kahoona's strong hand for support.

What I saw already came closer to the vision I had of that magical word: orgy.

The fire was still crackling but the boys had got up from their repose and they frizzled around with their coozies to the sound of Fats Domino's latest. I say frizzled because you couldn't very well call it dancing. First there was nothing but sand to support their feet and if there would have been more, the liberal intake of beer and vino had drained all the beef from the surfers' legs. They just rocked and rolled like crazy and it certainly was a far cry from the dancing old Pythagoras must have taught his disciples.

Someone grabbed me and hugged me close to his sweaty chest and it was a guy I had never seen before. You could tell he was in the last stages of delirium tremens. He could hardly hold you, no kidding. It was sort of disgusting, I must admit.

Of course, I looked out for Jeff and he had not changed position since I saw him last. He glowered at me and was obviously intent on stewing it out and stew it out he did. He was not real drunk or anything like that. He just slowly guzzled himself into a stupor.

Someone had the bright idea to hit out for the breakwater and do a little night-surfing. It was still so hot you thought the air would explode at the striking of a match. It was also incredibly dark. And a wind was blowing like something coming right out of a furnace.

One of the visiting guys had brought torches along, and he handed them around to anyone who wanted to go out for a night run. I saw Jeff getting up and grabbing one of them.

"Hold it, you guys," I heard the great Kahoona yelling. "You can't do this out here. We'll have the cops down in no time flat."

"Oh, kuk-i-nove the cops," yelled the fellow with the torches. He was a real grubby-looking guy with hairy legs.

Some nerve from an unknown. I expected the great Kahoona to put him in his place, but half a dozen of the fellows were already heading for the surf and Jeff was among them.

No one else paid any special attention—they kept on dancing. The phonograph was now giving out with some Hawaiian music and the crowd was snake-hipping around the fire, forehead to forehead. It was spooky and spectacular and real exciting.

The great Kahoona was chasing after the guys and I heard him scream, "Stop it, you crazy bastards!" But the crazy bastards didn't. Because of the darkness I couldn't watch them taking off, but I ran down to the surf and stood next to Cass and he kept on cursing in some island mumbo-jumbo and it was the first time I saw him getting really mad.

A few minutes later we were treated to a magnificent sight. All you could see were faraway specks of light but they came closer and fanned out as the hot wind roared from the sea with the speed of lightning. And the closer they came to the shore the more they fanned out and sparks of fire flew through the night. A couple of the boys must have got the axe because some fires were suddenly wiped out, but the few remaining came closer and the wind blew the sparks all over the place like on a Fourth of July jamboree.

The dancing had stopped and everybody now came rushing down to the dunes and kept yelling into the dark night like a bunch of crazy Comanches.

The ensuing events were sort of kaleidoscopic. I heard the guys yelling, I saw some of the surfers hitting the sand, and I saw Cass's face contorting itself into a horrified grimace as he heard some crackling sound behind him and quickly spun around.

"Good Christ!" he yelled. "Look, you stupid bastards!"

Now I saw it too. The sagebrush hills across the highway were on fire.

The last surfers, among them Jeff, had slithered onto the sand with a crunching sound. Now everyone stood rooted and we all stared at the hills where more and more little flames licked up and spread sideways until they gradually joined in a solid front. Obviously the wind had carried some of the sparks from the torches across, and in Southern California all that's needed to start a first-class holocaust is *one* small spark. We had learned this in school and now I looked at a genuine life-class demonstration.

In jig time the highway came to life. Cars started honking, people screaming, and the sound of approaching police cars and motorcycles roared through the darkness.

"Jesus Christ!"

"Dammit."

"Chrisamighty."

"Tough sh—"

They were all racing toward the hut, grabbing wildly for jeans and shirts and beach bags. The visiting coozies got the screaming meemies. They yelled their cute little peroxided heads off.

"Kill the fire," roared the great Kahoona, meaning the open fire with the suspended kettle of fish chowder. The crew dug their hands into the sand and poured it onto the fire, but before they could douse it a couple of uniformed men came racing down the path from the highway. They were game wardens and their flashlights exploded in our faces.

"What's going on here, you sons-of-bitches?" they screamed. "Who started that fire?"

What an asinine question!

Now you could hear the roar of fire engines pounding down the highway. They came from all sides—from the north and south . . . and some from the canyons. The heat was so intense that some of the rocks exploded.

"Let's get going, you guys," one of the wardens screamed. "They'll need firefighters."

"We have no equipment."

"It'll be up on the highway."

That was all the crew needed to hear. They bolted up the path leading to the highway, the girls racing after them. I caught a glimpse of Jeff. He was one of the last ones and before he panted after them he yelled at me: "Scram, Gidget, will you! Get home before they lock you up!"

Jeez. Why should they lock me up? I hadn't started anything. But my heart skipped a beat because he had thought of me.

I was the last one to scamper. I looked for my skirt and blouse but couldn't find them in that crazy mess-up. So I just ran up to the highway in my bathing suit.

The scramble on the main drag was something to behold. There was a conglomeration of uniforms, engines, red fire tanks, motorcycles, trucks, pumpers, bulldozers, huge searchlights, Red Cross canteens. People came running from the nearby motels and the restaurant on the pier and the Malibu Inn, and a loud-speaker boomed instructions, telling them to stay out of the way so the firemen could go to work.

The wind worked the fire uphill now and the firemen went after it with their hoses, but the fire seemed to be going a good deal faster than the fighters. The crew and their visitors had found a truck with equipment and they grabbed for axes and shovels and some other hardware I couldn't figure out, and they leaped over the ditches on to the hills and started hacking away like madmen.

I looked for my car and luckily I had it parked facing south, meaning homeways. I couldn't possibly have made a U-turn under the circumstances.

I took one more look at the holocaust before I settled down and started the motor. Okay, you crazy, mixed-up kid, I said to myself before I maneuvered myself out on to the highway, now you've been at a luau . . . now you know what an orgy looks like.

**Malibu, 1963. The beach
was getting crowded even then.**

Surf Photos by Grannis

Thirteen

I didn't get very far.

At the Malibu Sheriff Station they had set up a roadblock and I had to stop. They asked for my license and I told them I had lost it on the beach, which was the truth. The only thing I didn't tell them was that I only had a learner's licence and was not supposed to drive without escort.

"You park here and bring your licence back," the cop said.

"All right, if you insist," I consented.

And before you could say "Boo" to a goose I found myself hitchhiking back toward Malibu and the fire, barefoot and sans everything with my heart beating an irregular tattoo.

My poor guileless parents up at Lake Arrowhead! If they could have seen to what a degree of depravation their wayward daughter had sunk.

Some more engine trucks and police cars came racing by. One of the cars stopped and the officer asked me where I was heading for, so I told him that I was on my way home just down on the highway, and that I just had an ice cream soda at the drugstore. I have a faculty of lying that's simply way out.

When I finally reached the pier again, the police had roped off the highway for traffic and sightseers. Some of the girls from the luau stood around and they were sort of p.o.'d on account of being stuck there without transportation home.

The loudspeaker issued a running account of the progress of the fire, but all you could see was the faraway glow that gave the sky an eerie blue-red tinge.

Believe it or not, I suddenly started to shiver. The temperature must have been still in the eighties and the hot wind was still going something fierce. I stood there, thoroughly dehydrated. My skin must have had the pallor of bleached peanuts. My feet refused to function as organs of locomotion. Apparently there was no way of figuring how long it would take to get home unless I would have been willing to surrender to the nearest sheriff.

I was so tired I could have flopped down right on the pavement and gone to sleep. Probably some of the beer I had drunk worked on my metabolism or whatever it is that alcohol works on.

So I got the idea to take refuge at the beach. No one had roped off the path down to the Kahoona's hut. Maybe I would find my skirt and blouse. And maybe I could lie down on the cot and get some rest.

I sneaked away from the crowd and it was the best idea I had all evening. I found my stuff and all and the beach bag and I put the things on and went into the hut and flopped down on the cot. It was musty-smelling and pitch dark inside but I didn't mind.

I'm really not a callous person but at this moment I didn't care whether the damn fire would blow up all of Malibu in smoke, poof! I rolled myself up in one of the Kahoona's hairy blankets and was off in nod-land.

The next thing I knew was I felt like floating away on dark waters. Some dim shades emerged and were sucked up by the dark again and then some strange noises penetrated my ears and my hand shot to my face and it was wet. I opened my eyes and remembered instantly where I was but I also became aware that I wasn't alone in the hut.

It's silly, but the first thing I said into the darkness was, "What time is it?"—as if this had any importance. Then I sat up. Then I noticed why I was wet all over. Water came through the creases of the hut. It was raining.

"Who's here?" I said.

Someone lit the hurricane lamp. Now I recognized Cass. Some sight! The great Kahoona was covered with soot and smudge. His eyes had been far away but now that he recognized me, they came into focus again.

"If it isn't the Gidget," was the first thing he said.

"What's happened?" I said.

"Somebody up there liked us," grinned the great Kahoona. "We got some water from heaven. Rain, Angel. Didn't you feel it? Your face is all wet."

So that was it. It had rained. Something that might occur in Southern California once every decade had occurred that night. Talk of screwy coincidences!

"The fire," I asked. "What's happened to the fire?"

"Listen," the great Kahoona said.

I heard the faraway rumbling of departing trucks and motorcycles.

The great Kahoona struck another match and blew it out. "See," he said, "like that. The rain blew it out like that."

"Where are the fellows?"

"They went home."

"And it's all out? You put it all out?"

"The rain did it," said Cass, "just as it got close to some houses, it started. They already wanted to send some planes over. But the rain killed it. It was out in no time."

I felt so damn happy all of a sudden, glad for the Kahoona and the boys, glad it was all over and none of the houses had burned down.

Now the Kahoona looked at his grimy hands and face and he said: "I've got to wash up. Be right back."

"I'll fix you some coffee," I said.

I jumped up and got the coffee going. The hut had become my home by now. For a moment I thought it would be nice to keep house for Cass, to become a bum like him and establish a beachhead wherever some good waves were going, moving on to Makaha, Nanakuli or points west, just living from day to day, from minute to minute, being as happy as possible under the circumstances as they happen to you. For a moment I had even forgotten about Jeff.

The things that go on inside you when you're halfway between are just hair-raising, believe me.

Cass came back and I had the coffee going and now he looked

his normal self again, only a little tired from the hours fighting the fire.

We both drank the hot coffee and I told him how I happened to come back and fall asleep on his cot.

"That was right smart of you, Franzie."

"But I'd better be going now," I said and was all prepared to leave. He looked tired and I figured I'd walk up to the Sheriff's Station and show them my learner's permit. All I had to tell them was that my escort had got lost during the fire. If they locked me up I could always call Ann to bail me out.

"You can't leave now," said Cass. "It's the middle of the night."

"What time is it?"

"About three."

There was a pause.

"Why don't you go back to sleep some more?" said Cass.

"How about you?"

"I'll doze here in the chair."

I had never slept in one room with a man. Not to speak of a hut. I got frightened, naturally. Let's say I'd fall asleep. He might rape me. It had happened before. I could scream, but who would hear me?

My fingers began trembling, my pulse went rapidly. All kinds of thoughts raced through my head, some of them so startlingly romantic and biological that they surprised and shocked me. The next thought that rushed to my head was, what would happen if *I* invited him to lie down with me? That would sort of take the edge off. It'd be like brother and sister, just like playing house.

I waited.

As I was lying in the darkness I felt real alone and helpless like never before in all my fifteen years. There wasn't enough woman in me yet, and the gidget in me didn't know how to handle it. Will it always be like this, I thought unhappily, will I always be scared of it and scared of being scared?

What if I tried to let go? Maybe this was the right moment—maybe I would wake up in the morning and I would have become a woman overnight.

Jeez Louise, what a crazy notion. I tried to forget about it but the notion was with me to stay. A terrible longing grew in me. It grew to the point where I heard myself whispering, "Cass?"

He must have been wide awake because he replied instantly: "Yes, Angel?"

"Maybe you're not comfortable in that chair. There is room enough for both of us here."

Good God, I'd said it. I had hardly recognized my own voice.

I heard him get up and come over. He sat on the bed beside me. The most violent emotions were beating against me. And the surf pounding against the dunes was supplying the proper background music.

"You really want me to lie down with you?" Cass said now . . . very softly.

I still could say no. I wanted to say it, but what I really said was, "Of course."

Before I knew what was happening he was lying next to me. He slipped his arms around me . . . embracing me, my whole body.

It was shocking and overwhelming, feeling a man's body like

that. At this moment I knew that I had never lived at all. Maybe I
had not even been born yet. All my fears and frustrations seemed
to melt away in a sudden blaze.

Yes, this was the moment I had been waiting for.

Now it would happen. He would make me a woman.

And then I could have any man I wanted to. I could have Jeff.

Nothing happened.

After a while Cass said, "Ever slept hobo?"

"No," I whispered hotly. "How's that?"

"Just put your head on my shoulder, and I put my head on
your shoulder. Like this—

I felt his cheek against my cheek.

"I can hear your heart beating," Cass said.

"And I can hear yours."

I thought he would kiss me. But he didn't. We were lying
together like a man and a woman, but also like brother and sister.

"Franzie," he said after a long pause.

"Yes, Cass."

"You're a lovely girl, Franzie."

I didn't answer.

"I'm very fond of you, you know that, don't you?"

"Yes," I whispered.

"And you're in love with Jeff, aren't you?"

"I really don't know anymore," I said. I said the truth.

He drew me closer. My cheeks were on fire.

"Listen, Angel," he said. "You're everything a man would
ever want. You're sweet, you're young, and you're in love with
life. Remember this. So when it happens between you and a man
it must be beautiful."

I held my breath.

"And it must be all for love, Franzie. Not because you want to prove something to yourself. Not because you're impatient. The time must be ripe. When the time is ripe—you'll know. You'll be trembling the way you tremble now—but it'll be right. This isn't."

There was a long pause.

"I wish. . . . I could stay with you," I stammered.

"I would hurt you, Franzie."

"Have you been hurting Buff?"

"Buff and others."

Suddenly my face was wet again. But it wasn't the rain. I cried.

I didn't know why.

"It's tough to grow up," Cass said. "But it's also beautiful. Only you don't know it now. You'll know it one day."

Then he kissed me. He kissed me like a father. Different from Jeff. Tender.

After that we didn't speak. We did not move. I lay in drowsy stillness.

I had stopped crying. In a hazy way I understood what he had meant.

His body was still pressed against mine and a sense of peace fell over me.

I felt light.

I listened to the sound of the waves and then I fell asleep, our cheeks together.

"Shoot it, Gidget. Shoot the curl!!"

Surf Photos by Grannis

Fourteen

I must have been sleeping way into the morning, because when I opened my eyes the sun was filtering into the hut and I heard a roar from outside as if all hell was loose.

The great Kahoona was nowhere in sight.

My blouse and skirt looked a mess, all wrinkled up, and I decided to go out and have a morning swim before breakfast.

I slipped out of my clothes and threw them on the cot and just as I was about to head out, the door to the hut opened.

The sudden impact of the sun blinded me for a moment.

"Morning, Cass," I called out.

Anybody could have made that crazy mistake. The guy who stood in the door frame was almost as tall as Cass and he wore jeans and a T-shirt like him.

It wasn't the great operator, however. It was one of his sponsors. It was no other than Moondoggie.

But it wasn't only me who hadn't recognized him at first. There seemed to be something wrong with Jeff's eyesight too. He gazed about as if he couldn't focus very well, then he saw my skirt and blouse and I guess it was then that he recognized me.

"Gidget," he said flatly. "What in hell. . . ."

My mind was jumping around so quickly I hardly could keep track of it. Has he been looking for me? Did he think I had been sleeping with the great Kahoona? And if so, what would I tell him? I didn't know what to say so I just gave a fine imitation of a deaf mute and tried to brush past him and get outside.

"Hey, wait a moment—" He grabbed me by the wrist.

Well, here it comes, I thought.

"I want you to answer me."

"Why should I?" I said. "You didn't even talk to me last night."

"But now, *now* I want you to tell me—"

For a moment I felt an impulse to call for help, when I spotted the great Kahoona. He had just come out of the surf which was something tremendous. Waves about twenty feet high. That's the way it must look at Makaha at zero break, I thought. I wished I could have seen him come riding in. I had never seen them that bitchen, on my word of honor.

Jeff still had me by the wrist when the Kahoona came toward us, his board shouldered.

"Hi, man," he said, quite calmly. "What a surf!"

Only then he noticed the way Jeff was almost crushing my wrist. He didn't say anything. He put the board down and leaned it against the hut. Then of all things he started to whistle.

I guess it was the whistling that brought out the beast in Geoffrey Griffin. He released the grip on my wrist. I noticed that all the tan had faded from his face. It was real white now. He made a couple of steps towards Cass. His right fist traveled in a short arc and he hit the great Kahoona solidly on the chin.

"Jeff!" I yelled.

"Shut up," he yelled back.

Cass had stumbled, but it seemed as if the jab had merely shook him up a little. It also had cleared his head.

There was a moment of silence as those two giants faced each other. Then the Kahoona's face spread out like an accordion; he really laughed, and at the same time he hit back at Jeff with a haymaker that sent him backward, ricocheting into the wall of the hut. The Kahoona's surfboard started to sway and it would have crashed right down on Moondoggie if I hadn't had the presence of mind to hold out my hands and catch it at the last second.

Jeff stared up at the Kahoona. He was panting. And the Kahoona looked down at him and he kept smiling. And I stood there, gripping the surfboard in my hands, just staring.

Suddenly it hit me. I guess "like lighting" is too corny to write down but, Jeez, it fits to a T. It hit me that this wasn't a crummy movie I was watching. Two grown-up men had almost killed each other on account of little me—the gnomie, the shortie—the Gidget!

I noticed some blood trickling from Jeff's nose as he lay stymied and bleary-eyed against the wall of the hut, but instead of feeling compassion nothing but a pang of joy went through me. This was the pinnacle, this was the most. Surely nothing more wonderful would ever happen to me, ever.

Had I shouted they would certainly have thought I had gone crazy. So I did the next best thing to give vent to my soaring spirits. I lifted the board in my hands over my head and ran down to the water.

The board felt like feathers, all twenty-five pounds of it. The waves smashed against the dunes like one long, noisy, mad steamroller. I slid on the board and dug my hands into the water and shot over the foam like a speedboat. The cold water tingled about me sharp and like cold fire. A wave and another wave, high as houses, but I didn't care. Once I glanced back over my shoulder and saw Cass and Jeff. They had obviously run after me and they yelled something I couldn't hear and they waved their arms crazily, urging me to come back.

No, I wouldn't go back. Not for the life of me. The scenery had been all set up for me like an opening performance. This was the final testing ground I had picked for myself.

A few more strokes and I was beyond the surf-line. I couldn't see the coast any more, so high rose the wall of waves before me. I whirled around and brought the board in position. There was no waiting. I shot toward the first set of forming waves and rose.

I stood it. I have to come in standing, I told myself. I gritted my teeth.

"Shoot it," I yelled.

I was lifted up, sky high . . . and went down. But I stood it. One wave, another one.

"Olé!" I yelled. "Olé!"

Up I was—and down I went.

And still standing.

I was so jazzed up I didn't care whether I would break my neck or ever see Jeff again—or the great Kahoona.

I stood, high like on a mountain peak and dove down, but I stood it.

The only sound in the vast moving green was the hissing of the board over the water. A couple of times it almost dropped away under my feet, but I found it again and stood my ground.

"Shoot it, Gidget. Shoot the curl!!"

My own voice had broken away from me and I could only hear the echo coming from a great distance.

"Shoot it . . . shoot it . . . shoot it, Gidget!"

There was the shore, right there. I could almost reach out and touch it.

You're never too old to surf. This is Kathy at the beach in 1995.

Photo by Scott Starr—starr.photo@gte.net

Fifteen

Well, this is it.

This was the summer I wanted to write about, the memory of which I wouldn't part with for anything.

Now I'm middle-aged, going on seventeen. I've learned so much in between. I've learned that virtue has its points. That you can grow up even if you don't grow. That men are wonderful.

I'm beholden to the big operator ever since that night in August when he gave me a second helping of his profound philosophy. It's a quaint word, beholden, but that's what I am and I think Mister Glicksberg would appreciate my using it . . . more than many other words I have put down. That's why I'm not going to read these pages back. I might get red in the face and tear them up—the way I tore up the letter I once wrote to Jeff.

Oh, yes—we're writing steady now. He's shooting the curl at some bootcamp in Texas, being sponsored by the supreme commander himself. I got his fraternity pin before he left and, brother, do I make the most of it with those squares who think they're just *it*, because they have a few more inches upwards and sideways.

As for the great Kahoona, he had to fold up his stand after the fire and now he's probably pushing some green water down in Peru, operating with a new set of sponsors.

My big love is still out Malibuways with some bitchen surf going.

When it struck me this summer with Jeff it could have been just a dream. With Cass curiosity. But with the board and the sun and the waves it was for real.

All things considered—maybe I was just a woman in love with a surfboard.

It's as simple as that.

Kathy and her dad, Frederick Kohner, the author of <u>Gidget</u>, signing books and meeting the kids.

Photo courtesy of the Sun Valley News Bureau